THE
SECOND COMING
OF
LILITH

BOOK TWO

THE CHRONICLES OF LILITH

S.C. HELTON

ISBN: 978-1-956373-08-0 (sc)
ISBN: 978-1-956373-09-7 (hc)
ISBN: 978-1-956373-10-3 (e)

"I am more than half persuaded that I am a man's
soul put by some freak of nature into a woman's body…
because I have fallen in love with so many pretty
girls and never once the least bit with a man."

Louisa May Alcott

PROLOGUE

January 19, 2000

7:30pm

William Blockett picked Lily up for their date at exactly 7:30pm. No honking from the street with this young gentleman, no sir. He rang the bell and conversed with Lily's mom politely.

"I'll have her home by 11:00," he promised.

"Keep her out as late as you want," she said with a slur, "Jack has plans." She shuddered.

"Thank you, Mrs. Hardy."

"Your mom is a drunk," the young man opined, as they drove away.

"Thank you, Mr. Obvious," Lily replied.

The date went downhill from there.

9:00pm

Jack Hardy walked into his house with a girl he introduced as "Casey".

"Casey and I are going upstairs," he said.

There was no reaction from his wife, Beatrice.

"To fuck," he added.

Beatrice took a drink of bourbon, but her eyes never left the television.

"You're going with us," he said, venom dripping from his voice. He went and stood in front of his seated wife with his fists clenched.

"Oh, Fuck!" the girl called Casey thought.

As far as Casey was concerned, ***AMBUSHED!*** had jumped the shark early in the second season. The first season had been a hit with episode after episode of rich evangelical preachers getting caught with their pants down. The viewers loved it. They couldn't get enough. And that was the problem.

There are only so many sleezy hypocrites out there; and ***AMBUSHED!*** is a weekly show. That's where Casey and her colleagues came in. They dressed like whores, they looked like whores, and they acted like whores. They were "Producers".

The format of the show implies that housewives who suspect their husbands of cheating call in to the show. That happens, but not enough to keep the action going every week. That's where the 'producers' come in.

The producers hung out in bars and scouted for interesting married men. Ministers were best, but politicians, bankers, or doctors would do. The 'producer' would set up a rendezvous and alert her crew. When the no-good, philandering husband finally got around to doing what they had been manipulating him to do all night, the camera crew would rush in and catch him in the act. (Camera crews often took their time, in the hopes of catching the producer with her tits out.) Then the footage could be shown to the aggrieved wife, with predictable fireworks.

An upper-middle-class, big company boss like Jack Hardy was no blockbuster episode, but it would get respectable Neilson ratings. Casey's cameraman and sound man would rush in just as the dumbass was getting down to business, and there would be tears, confessions, promises of redemption, etc. The usual crap.

What "Crazy-eyes" was suggesting would get huge ratings. A threesome had never been done on network TV before! But where was the victim? The end of every episode was cathartic. The audience needed the victim's misery. Casey looked at the catatonic zombie staring blankly at a TV screen.

"This is not going to work," she thought, "The American public is sick, but not this sick."

What was playing out in front of her was all too familiar to her. She and her sister, Robin, had seen a relationship cross the Psychotic Threshold. They had witnessed the aftermath. It had ended with the murder/suicide of their parents. The scene, she knew, was leading to either a sick, pathetic sex tragedy, or violence. Her money was on violence.

"Hey, guys," she said, in a cheerful voice that sounded fake even to her, "I've got a couple of guys waiting for me just outside. They are big, burly guys, by the way…"

The guy looked at her. He looked exactly like Jack Nicholson looking through a splintered door, saying, "Here's Johnny!"

"Go upstairs and get in bed. We'll be up in a minute."

9:34pm

Billy had her bra off. He was squeezing her breasts and slobbering all over them. As long as he kept his hands above her waist, Lily was just sitting there, thinking of Scout.

She felt ridiculous. The fight had been all her fault. *"I mean, I know I'm gay,"* she said to herself as Billy suckled her like a 200lb. baby. *If Scout were touching my breast right now, with one finger, I'd be wet. I don't know why I can't just admit it to my parents. Well, yes, I do know why. My mom would cry, and my dad would probably kill me. Scout practically called me a coward, but she doesn't know my father. He beats mom all the time.*

A hand trying to sneak into her panties brought her back to reality.

"Bill, buddy, I've got some bad news. I'm gay."

9:55pm

The crazy man was blocking her exit out the front door. She retreated the only way she could… up the stairs.

"Yeah. You go on up and take your clothes off. Lay on your back with your legs spread. I'm going to watch my wife eat you out for a while. Prop yourself up on your elbows so you can suck me off when I tell you to."

Casey ran up the stairs. She went into the first room she came to. She called her cameraman.

"It's a NO-GO!" she screamed, "ABORT! Come get me out of here!

"We're at Denny's," the cameraman replied, "I just ordered a Belgian Waffle and Ray's got an All-American Slam. We'll pick you up in 30 or 40 minutes. Have fun!"

"Bastards!" Casey opened the door and looked out. Crazy Eyes had the lady's arm twisted behind her back and had forced her halfway up the stairs.

10:05pm

"It all goes back to my rejection of Alys," Beatrice mumbled. She was speaking out loud, but nobody was listening. Nobody had listened to Beatrice in years. "I denied Love because I was brainwashed into believing that true love could only exist between a man and a woman. Back then, girls like Alys were "Queers". I was cowardly and I denied Love. I deserve my misery. But, that girl at the top of the stairs has done nothing. I must protect her! I must stop him!

10:09pm

"I wouldn't piss on you if you were on fire," Billy Blockett said as he walked off.

"Thank you for a lovely evening," Lily replied. She opened the front door of her house and walked in. She saw her father choking a young woman at the top of the stairs. Her mother had her arms around his legs, trying to pull him back. She saw her father break loose of her mother and turn and kick her viciously. She tumbled down to landing halfway down the stairs. Lily ran up the stairs to defend her mother. She stood in front of her cowering mother.

10:11pm

Lily knew that all bullies are cowards. She had trained in martial arts since she was ten for just such an occasion as this. She knew that if a defender presented strength, the bully would usually back down. But there was something different about her father tonight. Perhaps he had ingested PCP, or his twisted mind had finally snapped, but she saw madness in those wild eyes.

"Get out of the way, Lily. I'm going to kill her this time." He lunged.

Lily threw him over the railing to the marble floor below.

10:16pm

Casey Reynolds, Beatrice Hardy, and Lily Hardy looked down at the lifeless body of Jack Hardy.

"Oh, my God! I've murdered him." Lily said.

10:18pm

"You two get out of here." Beatrice said. "I'll handle this."

"Mom, I think we should call the police."

"Listen to your mom," Casey said, taking Lily's hand and pulling her toward the door. "I only knew your father for three hours, but I know he was not a nice person. He shouldn't be allowed, even posthumously, to mess up the life of a good kid like you. Come with me and let your mom deal with it."

As Casey pulled her out the front door, Lily heard her mom say, "Thank you, Lily."

"Where are we going?" Lily asked.

Casey held a finger up in a 'just a minute' sign and spoke on the phone, "Way to go, Jag-off! The guy went psycho and almost killed me! Now listen, we cruised the bars for talent until eight o'clock and gave up and went home. You dropped me off before ten, got it?"

"My car's at the airport." Lily said.

Casey held another finger up. "Robyn, I can barely hear you. Are you guys having a party? A gig? How long are you going to be in town? Perfect! Can you give a friend of mine a lift? To wherever you're going. OK, see you in an hour."

Hanging up the phone, Casey asked, "How would you like to join a band?"

CHAPTER ONE

DAWN LIGHTS UP MY DAY

When they tried to kill me back in 1990 and killed Nan Butler instead, I just kinda checked out. To paraphrase the Beatles, I spent four or five years "sucking my thumb and wandering by the banks of my own lagoon". I hated this world. Our world was a place where "the good die young" was an accepted bromide, and the largest religion used an instrument of torture as its symbol.

Religion and politics had turned our earthly paradise into hell itself. It had driven me quite mad. Before Nan was killed saving my life, I was convinced I could hear the disembodied voice of Lilith, Original Mother of Humanity. As some pompous religious figure eulogized Nan, Lilith whispered in my ear:

"Twas a far, far better thing.."

"SHUT THE FUCK UP!" I screamed.

Right there, in the middle of Nan's funeral, I completely lost it. I was screaming at my incorporeal spiritual guide as loud as I could:

"Nobody gives a shit about you, Lilith. Nobody cares about Zeus or Thor or Buddha, or Mohammed! Frankly, we are all wondering if Jesus has missed the bus, too.

They locked me up in an insane asylum after that, but, at least, Lilith never bothered me again. Finally, my therapist, a fellow inmate named Chico Josephson, convinced me that if I stayed away from politics and religion; I could be a useful, functioning member of the human race. So, I got myself a steady job.

My friend Martha, the most beautiful straight girl in the world, had started up a Bond Recovery Service. She and Starr and Aggie and Irene were all Bounty-Hunters! When I joined them in 1995, we chased the really bad dudes, like rapists, murderers, and government officials. Over the years, though, we've become specialists. We focus on runaways and missing children, now. Since all of us except Martha are lesbians, the business is named Sappho Security Services.

Aggie and Irene quit soon after I joined. They swore it had nothing to do with me. Irene's dad, Lawrence Worthinghampton, had offered Irene control of the Worthinghampton Orphanage and the Third Eye Academy that served as its school. Aggie swore it had nothing to do with the time she caught Irene and me in a compromising position. Irene was thirteen at the time and it was very embarrassing for me.[1]

Martha tapped on the frame of my open door. "Someone here to see you," she said.

I looked up in exasperation. I was in the middle of a particularly difficult crossword puzzle and did not welcome any interruptions. That is one of the perks of being nuts. No one wants to hire a crazy bounty hunter. I get to goof off all day while others do all the work. Before I could think of a smart-ass reply, I saw who was behind her.

"Dawn!" I jumped up and ran across the office to hug her.

You might think that I would react negatively to seeing Dawn, since the first time I saw her, she was holding Nan's dying body in her arms. Counterintuitively, I was delighted every time I saw Dawn. She reminded me of the living Nan. She was funny and kind, and always trying to help someone. Dawn didn't look anything like Nan (Well, she was white, for one thing), but she always reminded me of her.

---

[1] Irene later confessed that she intentionally seduced me, not because she was interested in me sexually, but because she wanted to see if she could wield power over people the way her daddy did. It's an interesting story and maybe I'll tell it later, but, right now, just believe me, I'm not a gay pedophile.

Dawn looked on my desk and saw the unfinished crossword puzzle.

"Working on today's crossword, huh?" she asked, "I tried to do it earlier, but I couldn't come up with a 7-letter-word that starts with an 'O' and means *easily understood or perceived*."

"It's 'OBVIOUS'."

"Maybe for you, but I couldn't figure it out."

"Hey, Dawn. How about this view?"

Sappho Security Service had come a long way since the office was the bedroom in my grandmother's house. It had been ten years since we first saw Mr. W's lake cabin. It had been huge, then. Now it was a Five-Star Hotel. We had our own suite on the fourth floor. My office window actually faced the back, away from the view of the lake; but I could see straight across to the Worthinghampton Orphanage. The Worthinghampton Buddhist Temple had been moved here to the hill, years before. It had shut down when Irene decided she would rather be Aggie's partner than a Buddhist monk. What was left of the temple had been rebuilt into an orphanage. Later, the *Third Eye Academy* had been added to provide an education for the orphans.

"What brings you to Sappho Security Services?" I asked.

"I heard something that might interest you, Alys. I got a 'heads up' from one of my classmates at TCU. There's a cheerleader that's apparently gone missing."

"I don't chase TCU cheerleaders anymore, Dawn. And if I did, I wouldn't kidnap them."

"I'm just saying, a twenty-two-year-old girl has disappeared under suspicious circumstances. They're putting up pictures all over campus. The girl's name is Lily. Someone said she had a mother named Beatrice who knows you.

Stanley Scovall looked up when District Attorney, Virgil Wilder, walked in. "If it's not good news, I don't want to hear it," he said.

"Well, its good news and bad new," Virgil Wilder said. "The good news is that Texas' newest Senator is mixed up in a scandal. The bad news is that she's only peripherally involved, and the next election is two years away. It will all be forgotten by 2002. Still, I thought you might want to see this," she said, throwing a copy of *SPYGLASS* on the desk.

SPYGLASS was a gossip rag that hoped to be the *NATIONAL ENQUIRER* when it grew up. It was delivered to supermarkets all over Fort Worth by over-achieving Journalism majors each week.

Above the fold, on the front page, was a picture of Starr Williams with her arm around a younger lady. The two were gazing at each other with unabashed desire. The caption read:

Starr Williams, long-time associate of State Senator Cathy Anderson celebrates "Gay Pride Week" with a young lady who gave her name as "Lucky Betts".

In 2000, even legitimate news outlets hesitated to use the words "girlfriend" or "partner" when describing a relationship between two women. People who followed State politics, however, understood what "long-time associate" meant. Starr and Cathy had been together since Cathy entered Texas politics.

"This could definitely bite Cathy on the ass," Stanley predicted.

"I don't think so, sir. Voters in Tarrant County consider Cathy a hard-working State Senator who has been too busy to find 'Mr. Right'. They have no idea of her sexual peccadillos."

"We could tell 'em."

"Let's keep that in our back pocket for now, sir. I want to defeat Cathy in the next election and become the State Senator from District 10; but I want to put Alys Loxley in jail *right now*. I've hated her ever since she bloodied my nose and broke my heart in high school. I think what she's doing with those runaways is criminal and unamerican. I want to destroy that bitch."

Stanley was examining the photograph closely. "I know the camera probably caught them unaware, but look at the pose it caught them in. The girl is on the arm of Starr's chair and Starr's arm disappears behind the girl's back. What does that say to you?"

"Starr Williams is a lesbo?"

"I'll tell you what it looks like to me. It looks like Starr's got herself a life-size puppet. She's got her hand in the girl's back, controlling her. Wouldn't it be funny if the Mystery Lady's name were Mortimer Snerd?"

In actual fact, the Mystery Lady's name was **not** Mortimer Snerd. It was Lucky. Lucky's mother was, unquestionably, the Poster Child for Sterilization.

Mabel Betts started going to Thursday Night Bingo at the VFW with her grandmother when she was eleven. She loved it. Then, in no particular order, she learned to love poker, craps, roulette, blackjack, horses, and the lottery.

On the day her daughter was born, "Montezuma's Revenge" had come in at 20-1 earning her $2000. Thus, "Lucky" received her unfortunate moniker. In school, she tried to get kids to call her "Lucy", but everyone knew that her mother was an inveterate gambler and the name stuck like an ugly wart.

When Lucky was twelve, she read a book called *Reincarnation and Karma* by Edgar Cayce. Lucky had never felt any familial connection to her parents. She felt like she did not belong with them. She felt like she had been dropped out of an airplane onto a primitive tribe. Once she read Cayce's book, she understood. In some previous life, she had done something awful, and her current life was her karmic punishment.

Lucky became an astrologer. She charted the stars and sought her fate. She knew her hero would find her and save her from her miserable life. She kept her eyes open and worked hard. By the time she was twenty, she had her own Fortune Telling business on Denton Hwy. in Haltom City, TX.

One night a limo pulled into the driveway. A big man in a black suit got out and entered the front door. He nodded at her, looked around, checked the back room, and left. A minute later, two women came in and sat down. She offered a Tarot reading, but they had specific questions they wanted answered.

One was tipsy, and the other was itching for a fight. Lucky didn't need the ten dollars she got for a reading badly enough to get in the middle of a fight, so she asked for payment up front. Sometimes that puts the customer off and they will leave.

No such luck with these two. The tipsy one took out her purse. When she opened it up, Lucky noticed several pictures of a child, but what caught her attention was a receipt from "Glenview Animal Clinic". She couldn't see the name of the animal, or even if it were a dog or a cat. What she could clearly see was the total amount of the bill: $1495.75. It was marked- Paid in Full!

"Somebody loves little Bowser," she thought.

The ladies were easy to read. They were obviously a couple, although they were going to great lengths to pretend they were a couple of straight girls out looking for guys. The angry one was a knock-out beauty, but to Lucky's trained eye, was just four or five years from a major fade-out. The tipsy one seemed to Lucky to be a free spirit, one of those thirty-something ladies who 'just wanted to have fun'. This is the kind of woman Lucky would like to hang out with, if Lucky ever hung out. (Which she didn't.)

"I want to know," Tipsy asked, "if the man of my dreams is out there."

"And I want to know," Angry said, "if I committed to the wrong person."

Standard Operating Procedure in a case like this was to spout bland generalities until the drunk gets bored and the angry person gets pissed and they leave. But Lucky didn't know many people who could pay $1500 for a sick pet. She wanted to know more about this couple.

"Are you sure," she asked Tipsy, "that the man of your dreams is a man?" Then, without waiting for an answer, she asked Angry, "If you DID commit to the wrong person, who is the right person?"

"Alys," Tipsy answered for Angry.

One didn't need ESP to sense the tension in the room. Lucky noticed some tiny, white hairs on Angry's lap. Small dog or cat? Lucky took the 50/50 shot. "Is your cat feeling better?"

Angry's eyes brightened. For the first time, she smiled. She was even more beautiful.

"The vet says Zonker could live many more years with the proper care. Won't you pray for her?

Such mewling solicitousness did not come naturally to Cathy. Ten years in Texas politics had taught her that Texans believe in reliance on prayer. (If not its efficacy; hence, "Oh, you have Class 4 cancer? Our prayers are with you." Or "Oh, you want the Cowboys to win a Super Bowl in your lifetime? We'll pray for you.")

Lucky was suddenly very tired. Her line of work shielded her from the harsh realities of Capitalism and Christianity most of the time. People came to her seeking the magical and mystical. She didn't have to think often of people spending $1500 to keep a cat alive a year or two past its natural lifespan while human beings rummaged through the dumpster of the bakery next door for bread. And now this woman wanted her to intercede with Divinity on behalf of her fat cat?

"Fuck Zonkers," she said with a sigh, "I hate cats."

Angry got up and walked to the door. "You coming, Starr?"

Tipsy was scribbling on the back of a "Psychic's for All Occasions" brochure.

"Be right there, Cathy."

She scribbled a few more words; then said, "You were great, Lilith, very helpful." (Lucky hated her real name and had a nametag that said "Lilith".)

When they had left, Lucky read the writing on the back of the pamphlet:

> "I hate cats, too. Zonker belongs to my adopted daughter.
> Her name is Chloe. Meet me at Riscky's in the stockyards
> tomorrow at 8:00 PM. My name is Starr.
>
> P.S. What do you call a psychic midget who has escaped
> from prison?"

Dawn Hightower would have known the answer: "A small Medium at large." Dawn liked jokes. One thing she <u>didn't</u> like was interviewing a bunch of cheerleaders.

"Alys would love this," Dawn thought, "All these pretty girls in various stages of undress would be heaven for Alys. Perhaps *SHE* should be the criminology major trying to get a job as a policeperson."

"I'm all for diversity," Cyndi told Dawn, "I think the squad should have a gay or two, as long as they're pretty. I just think Lily overdid the 'butch' thing. I mean, you could **see** her biceps bulging, for Heaven's Sake! She thought she was so tough because she could beat up boys. She once gave my boyfriend, Gary, a black eye when he supposedly touched her breast. Ha, fat chance! Like he said, "Why should I want to touch her tiny melons, when yours are so huge?"

Cyndi seemed to think that if she shoved the boobs in question into Dawn's face, Dawn would be able to see the wisdom of her boyfriend's choice.

Dawn took a step back and asked, "Have you seen her since January 19th?"

"I haven't seen her since coach assigned her to the base of the pyramid, you know, with all the cows. I think that was Coach's way of saying, "Strong arms will not get you to the top of the pyramid.""

"Very well put, Cyndi. Very profound. So, you have no idea what may have happened to her?"

"For all I know, she might have been kidnapped by a roaming band of lesbian witches."

Strangely enough, Cyndi had hit the nail right on the head! Lily had been handed over by that hard-working muckraker, Casey Reynolds, to her sister, Robyn, better known as 'Marian," of **Marian and the Merry Maidens**. The band was on its way to Seattle in a psychedelically painted minivan. They were headed home to their base; a club called <u>The Corner Coven</u>. Lily had gotten a contact high from all the marijuana being passed around, and had forgotten, quite frankly, about her girlfriend, Scout, until they were halfway across Ohio.

Then, she couldn't find her phone. When she borrowed Janet's, she couldn't remember the number. "It's OK," Lily told the teenage girl who had crawled onto her lap, "Scout is probably still pissed about the whole 'Mascot Incident'[2].

Who's pissed?" the drummer, Kitty, asked.

"Good point," Lily said, and fell asleep.

Misty woke Lily up with kisses. For a fifteen-year-old, she was quite adroit. She kissed Lily's sweaty neck and moved up to her jawline. With her lips barely touching Lily's skin, she kissed one cheek, up over the nose, and on to the other cheek. It wasn't until Misty was sucking on her lower lip that Lily admitted to being awake.

"What's up, kid?"

"We're here," Misty said, "Get up and see our new home for the next three weeks."

The Coven was a dump. At least, at 8:00 AM in the morning it was. There was hot coffee, though, thanks to the owner, Kate Culpepper.

"Welcome girls," she said, and gave each a hug and a kiss. There was no kiss when she got to Lily and the hug was perfunctory.

"You're new."

"I'm not actually a member of the band."

"She's our Mascot," Misty said, jumping up and down, "She tore a pony's head off!"

"Listen up, everybody," Robyn said, "Janet and I are going home. We'll be back at 8:00 for our gig tonight. Misty, call your mom to come get you."

Robyn looked at Lily and said, "Liz has arranged to bunk here with Kate. If you want to stay a while, you're welcome. Otherwise, have a good life."

Kate pulled Robyn aside and whispered in her ear. Lily heard Robyn whisper "Shit". Then she said, "Alright Misty. Your mom is sick again. You can come home with Janet and me."

---

[2] The Mascot Incident: Lily caught the SMU mascot flirting with Scout. She said they were 'hugging and shit'. The SMU mascot is a pony. Lily ripped the pony's head off and ran down the field with it. Many SMU players tried to stop her. She amazed 32,000 fans when she STIFF-ARMED a 330 lb. guard, ran the pony head the length of the field to the TCU goal line and, spiking the head, proceeded to imitate a male urinating on it.

Nobody seemed happy with that, least of all, Janet.

"It's OK," Misty said, "I'll stay here with Kate." Kate gave the girl another hug.

Robyn looked at Lily and said, "A word?"

It was a question, but not one Lily could refuse.

"First, take this," she said, handing Lily her phone. "You didn't lose it; although, you DID throw up on it once. We confiscated it on orders from my sister, Casey. It seems there was some bad shit going down there and your mom wanted you well out of it. She told the police that you confessed to being a homosexual and she threw you out hours before your father came home."

"But I never got around to telling her. How did she know?"

Robyn smiled sympathetically. "Sometimes moms know more than we think."

"In the meantime," Robyn continued, "Misty is a 'special needs' kid. She's been exposed to sexual promiscuity since she was a baby. Nevertheless, she's a fourteen-year-old kid under our protection. Get it?"

"Copy that. What's wrong with her mom?"

"Overdose. She'll be in the hospital for a while." She paused. "The thing is, Lily; Janet and I are like mom and dad to Liz and Misty. We've been on the road for six weeks, and Janet and I would like a little 'alone' time, you know? If you could take them under your wing for a day or two, we would really appreciate it."

"Glad to do it."

"Just remember: If you hurt her in any way, you'll answer to me."

"No worries, Robyn. My girlfriend is a Senator's nanny. I know how to take care of kids."

"Yeah, I saw last night. That's what I'm worried about."

"Hey, I didn't know she was fourteen. And I have no idea what might have happened. There were some powerful fumes in that van. Don't worry, Robyn. I got this."

Lily offered to serve drinks or wash glasses, but Kate Culpepper made it clear she only wanted Lily to watch Liz and Misty and keep them out of trouble. The three of them found the light room where different kinds of lights were projected onto the dance floor during

Merry Maidens performances. From that concealed room, they could see the entire bar.

The clientele consisted largely of students from the nearby University of Washington. It reminded Lily of bars in the TCU area back home. A moment of homesickness enveloped her, but she quickly shook it off. This trip to the west coast was a huge adventure and she was beginning to have fun. She didn't want to think about the past.

"Why is it called The Coven?" she asked.

Liz said, "They say in the old days, most of the customers were local Wiccans. Then the students took over and the old witches declared the place 'déclassé'."

"Phillipa still comes sometimes." Misty said.

"She better not," Kitty said, heatedly. "Kate will poison her drink!"

"Who's Phillipa?" Lily asked.

"She's…"

"Nobody."

The girls spoke at the same time, then looked uncomfortable and stopped speaking.

"I gotta go," Misty said, and went upstairs where they were bunking.

"Is she alright?" Lily asked.

"She had a crush on a very powerful witch. It didn't go well. She still has nightmares. I better go make sure she's OK."

When she was alone, Lily watched the crowd grow in the Coven. Many of the couples were in their twenties, like her and Scout. She thought about Scout. It had only been three days since she had seen her, but, somehow, she already seemed to belong to the past: back there with her father. She was on a new journey, now, and she wondered where it would lead.

CHAPTER TWO

A Fairy Tale with a Curse

Fort Worth football fans remember Nov. 26, 1999 as the day that TCU brought home the 'Iron Skillet' by defeating SMU 21-0. Lily Inouye will remember it as the day she almost peed herself in front of 30,929 people.

It's not easy to look good in purple and white, but the TCU cheerleaders pulled it off. As the exotic Polynesian beauty down on the end, Lily felt conspicuous and hated to leave the game for *personal* reasons. She almost waited too long. Finally, with 3:17 left in the second quarter, she was able to slip away and take care of business.

Ten minutes later, greatly relieved, she headed back towards the field. She passed a dark cul-de-sac under the bleachers, behind some refreshment stands.

"Stop it, Danny! Please stop. I said, 'NO'!

"This is it!" Lily thought to herself, *"This is the day I've been preparing for since I was six. Hiding in that closet, listening to my mother being beaten, I swore someday I'd be big enough to fight back.* **This** *is why I took Jiu Jitsu lessons for ten years."*

For Lily, a lifetime of fear and impotence was about to end. Her fight against bullies was about to begin. Lily leapt over the four-foot fence that separated the food booths from the footpaths. A big, musclebound ape in a TCU jersey was holding a small black girl down on the dirty concrete.

The big ape looked over his shoulder and said, "Fuck off, cunt."

Lily picked up a brick that had been holding a door open and advanced toward her target. The big oaf made two strategic errors. He said, "Wait a minute", and tried to buckle his pants.

Lily walked up to him and smashed the brick into the side of his head just above the ear. He hit the ground like a ton of bricks. A second later, so did the brick.

"He thought I would sacrifice my tactical advantage and negotiate," she later explained to Scout.

"The authorities treat criminals like debutantes these days, they read them their rights, make sure their civil liberties are protected, even make sure they don't bump their heads when they put them in a police car. Criminals expect to be treated with respect. They need to learn that they are scum and will be punished for their crimes."

The little girl was rearranging her clothes as she ran. She ran into the open booth and began pulling cash out of the registers.

"Hey, wait a minute," Lily said, "shouldn't we report this?"

"I was working off the books," Scout said. She looked at Lily and wondered if the Hawaiian girl understood the idiom. "Under the table?" she tried. "Nontaxable?" She finished stuffing her bag and said impatiently, "He owes me this, you get it?"

She leapt over the bar of the booth and headed down the mezzanine. Lily calmly lifted the hinged part of the bar and followed the girl. The girl was extraordinarily beautiful and fascinating, but Lily wasn't going to get caught up in a robbery.

"But what if I already have?" she thought, *"When that guy wakes up, he's going to say he was beaten and robbed by two girls, a black girl and a Polynesian TCU cheerleader. How hard will it be for the cops to find a Polynesian cheerleader here? I better find out who this chick is so I can establish an alibi."*

Lily's worries were forgotten for a moment as she tried to imagine a line-up of cheerleaders. Instead of avoiding eye-contact and trying to blend into the background; the girls would be vying for attention. They would be shaking their pom-poms and kicking their legs high, yelling, "Pick me. Pick me."

"I'm just going to brazen it out," she decided. Now that she had finally acted, now that she had fought back against bullies, she felt brave.

She followed, as the girl made her way out of the stadium without incident. There was an area out front where, in a few hours, buses would pick up SMU students and take them back to Dallas. A black Lincoln Town Car pulled up where the girl waited. A dark-haired lady got out and ran to her.

"Are you alright, Scout?"

"I'm OK, Starr. Let's go."

That was all Lily heard. The two got in the car and it drove off. Lily wrote down the license number.

It wasn't difficult tracking down the Snack Booth Girl. The plates of the Town Car were State Government plates. The car was being used by State Senator Cathy Anderson.

Going on the internet at the Fort Worth Library, Lily found some pictures of the woman the girl had called Starr. In one, she stood next to a girl. The caption read, "Senator Anderson's Personal Assistant and her stepdaughter enjoy the annual Easter Egg Hunt in Burnett Park." Standing close by was the girl the lady had called 'Scout'.

Lily learned that Cathy Anderson had been Mayor of Fort Worth before running for state Senator and winning. Her personal assistant, in those days, had been Starr Williams. Starr had adopted a girl. The girl's nanny was the girl that Lily had rescued. Her name was Scout.

Lily caught up to Scout as she was dropping off Chloe at the "One Eye Acadamy.

"Hi, I'm Lily. You remember? From the game?"

"Great to meet you, Lily. Are you here for your half of the take?"

Lily was so taken aback, she couldn't speak.

Scout laughed. "Just kidding. I just didn't expect to ever see you again. I felt bad when I got home and realized I didn't even thank you for saving me from that animal, Danny. He would have raped me for sure if you hadn't come along."

Lily looked down at the girl next to Scout, uncomfortably.

"Oh, don't worry about Chloe. She's some kind of child prodigy. She may not be able to imagine the horror of rape, but she can recite the dictionary definition."

"Forcible Sexual Intercourse," the girl said.

Scout looked upward and mumbled, "Insufferable little twat."

Chloe put her hands on her hips and said, "I could have you fired for that."

"Go to class," Scout said, wearily.

"You're supposed to escort me to the door."

Scout pretended to take a swing at the girl, and she scooted off to class.

"Want a cup of coffee?" Scout offered.

"Sure."

They drank their coffee in the school cafeteria.

"I can't leave the premises," Scout told Lily. "I'm not only her nanny, I'm her bodyguard as well. It's not just her proximity to a State Senator that's potentially dangerous. She's a child evangelist and has enemies of her own."

"What about you? Is Danny a danger to you?"

"No, he won't cross the Senator. He'll slink away like the creep he is. I was just working for him for some easy cash. What are you smiling about?"

"Sorry. I just can't imagine someone like you needing cash. I can't imagine what for. Surely, you don't have a gambling problem?"

"No, and don't call me 'Shirley'.

They laughed and, after a comfortable silence, Scout said, "You know, you saved my life and I find I quite like you and trust you, so I'm going to answer that question. I'll answer it with another question:

"What does a nanny do when her charge becomes an adult?"

"Find another kid?"

"Right. Unless your mom died in prison for killing your father and your grandmother is a Voo-Doo witch doctor. It doesn't look good on a resume."

"No, I guess not. I'm surprised you even got the job you have now."

Before my mom was sent to prison, her best friend was Alys Loxley, the writer. You ever heard of her?"

"No, I can't say I have."

"Well, apparently she and mom were very close." Scout paused to see if Lily would make some kind of salacious remark about just how close they were, but Lily's mind doesn't work that way, so she continued. "When my mom found out she was dying, she made Alys promise she would take care of me. Alys got me the job of nanny to Starr's kid, but this kid is growing up fast. Frankly, she doesn't need me now. In two or three years, I'm going to need a new career. Hence my need for a stake."

"Tell you what. I'm going to be a crime-fighting Superhero. I may have an opening for a sidekick."

"What do the uniforms look like?"

The two talked all day. When the bell rang for Chloe to get out, Lily suddenly got serious. "I know I've only known you for a brief time, but I feel like I have to tell you; Scout Blanchard, I love you!"

"That's OK. Don't worry about it. That happens to me all the time. It's the 'Blanchard Curse'.

Martha was trying to act casual. She came into my office with the projections for the 2001 budget. Nothing wrong with that except I wouldn't need them for another six months.

"Oh, by the way," she said, in a Super-Fake offhanded way, "There's someone here to see you."

"That someone have a name?" I asked.

"Name's Starr," Starr said from the doorway.

I had long since forgiven Starr for choosing Cathy over me. Nobody's perfect. Some observers, with all the facts at hand, might even say it was my own fault. The near-perfect love affair between Nan and me, so tragically interrupted, had left me philosophical about such things; and the sight of my former lover always made me a little sad, but without enmity.

"Guards, have this riff-raff thrown to the dogs."

"It's good to see you, too, Alys."

"What do you want, Starr?"

"I would like you to go to a tent revival with me at Sagamore Baptist Church."

"I've heard your stepdaughter preach before, Starr. She's as sweet as can be, but she's not my cup of tea."

"Her message has changed recently. It's darker. I don't know where she's coming up with this stuff. Come on, Alys. She won't listen to me. See if you can talk some sense into her."

When Amy Dunnally died, her twelve-year-old daughter was sent to Worthinghampton Orphanage. No one knew who the father was. Stanley swore it wasn't his. She had been in Switzerland getting treatment from a renowned brain specialist in 1988. When she came back, she had the baby with her.

Starr thought the baby was adorable, (plus she felt guilty for Amy's unhappiness) so, in 1990, she adopted the two-year-old girl.

Chloe had been a child evangelist since the age of seven. She couldn't be seen standing behind the pulpit at first, so she strutted back and forth across the stage, holding a Bible. She wore a long, white robe (like a little angel) and, incongruously, cowboy boots. Her blonde hair fell to her waist. Many of the congregation thought she looked "just as cute as a bug's ear".

She preached a big ol' Texas-size heaven. Every blessed soul owned their own world. You could eat Sweet Tarts for breakfast and cotton candy for lunch. You could have streets of gold if you wanted them, and there were plenty of servants to fix your favorite meals whenever you wanted.

"Just make sure your tithes are all paid up when you reach those Pearly Gates," she would warn with a cute little pearly smile on her face."

Starr was right. Her message was darker, now.

"A young woman stands before you today, but the words she speaks come from your Creator. Your Creator is angry! For 2000 years, a lie has been perpetrated about My creation; and I have chosen this young lady to reveal the truth to you.

"I DID NOT create Adam and Eve. I created Adam and LILITH!

"I created them both from the same clay. I created them as equals! I created a Perfect World, and then, I moved on. I had other worlds to create.

Then that sniveling Adam came round pulling on my dress and whining about his partner wanting to be on top during procreation. I checked the manual and I told him:

"BEHOLD! Verily, it works either way!"

But the schmuck kept pestering me about his 'dignity' and being formed in My Image.

"What do you know of My Image? You have never seen me. If you ever saw me, your head would explode!"

"But what's a Deity to do, right? I mean, the customer is always right, yeah?

"So, I made Eve. Not one of my better works: servile, obedient, and meek. Good characteristics in a lap dog. But who wants a lap dog for a wife?

"Listen, I've put up with it for 2000 years, but even MY patience has limits. I've decided that on Lilith's 333rd reincarnation, I'm going to give her Self-Realization.

(Not all-at-once of course, I don't want to kill her!) Little by little, she will remember every lifetime she's lived and all the magic I ever gave her."

"And I'll tell you something else! God can use all the exclamation marks that God wants! God can use two, if God wants!! You got a problem with that?"

I met Chloe after the sermon and said, "Nice show."

"I know you are, but what am I?"

Child-prodigy she may be but she's still a little brat.

CHAPTER THREE

Asymmetric Warfare

"So, what did you think?" Starr asked me after Chloe's sermon.

"Well, at least she didn't do the bit about 'Blacks' having their own heaven," I said, "but I do agree she's a lot darker these days. What crawled up her ass?"

"Well, you remember when you were, um…"

"Wandering the banks of my own lagoon?"

"Yeah, I was going to say when you were checked into the "Happy Hotel", but yeah, then.

Everybody talked for years about how you cracked up at Nan's funeral. Some said it sounded like you had been possessed by Lilith and had exorcised her right there."

"Starr, I don't really like to think, much less talk, about those days, but suffice it to say that that was basically what happened."

"OK, yeah. I get it. So, then, there were naturally those who were asking: "So, where did she go? Meaning Lilith, you know?"

"Yeah, so?"

"Well, I think Chloe plans on cashing in on that. I think she wants people to think she is the new voice of Lilith."

"Be careful what you wish for."

"Yeah, well, here's the thing: just between you, me, and her eight million listeners; Chloe started her period last month."

"Too much information."

"Chloe is concerned (and rightfully so, I think) that the trajectory of a child-evangelist's career will follow that of the child actor. Adulthood means obscurity. She thinks she needs a new act."

"You mean like the whole Hanna Montana/Miley Cyrus thing (without the pole-dancing)."

"Who is Hannah Montana, or Miley Cyrus? What is 'pole-dancing'?"

"Sorry. That hasn't happened yet in this universe. Forget it." (That's one of the hazards of hanging with Lilith. Her experiences are not necessarily chronologically linear.)

"You remember Zana contesting the results of the election, don't you?" Starr asked me.

"Election?"

"Jesus, Alys! Work with me here. You ran against Cathy for High Priestess of the Dianic Wiccan Church of Lilith. Before the results were announced, Evie Longorgeous tried to assassinate you. You never had the chance to address the full membership and Zana contested the results of the election. It caused a schism in the church that continues to this day. Does any of that ring a bell?"

"Zana is Nan's younger sister, isn't she? How's she holding up?"

"For fuck's sake, Alys, it's been ten years! She is fine. She is the High Priestess of the Church of Lilith."

"So, I guess Cathy is the High Priestess of the other one, The Diane Wicca Church?"

"God, Alys. Cathy lost her religion in 1994, when she became Mayor of Fort Worth."

"How are you and her getting along?"

"None of your goddamn business and don't believe everything you read in the *Spyglass*."

"She's got you tied to the whipping post, don't she, girl?"

"Alys, don't."

"Makes you dress up just right and attend all those fancy parties."

"Alys, stop."

"Keeps you on a leash and shows you off to all her friends, huh?"

I went for the left feint, and she got me with a powerful right roundhouse. I saw stars and heard a ringing in my poor, red ear.

You still can't fight for shit," Starr said, rubbing her knuckles.

"Well, I'm glad you two are still getting along," I said, after a while. "So, if Cathy's left the church to pursue a career in politics; who's the other High Priestess?"

"That's what I'm trying to tell you, Alys. If we don't do something, it'll be Chloe Dunnally/Williams.

Celeste Worthinghampton planned on fighting an asymmetric war against men. There would be no Front, no battlelines, just the lightning-fast strike here and there at any time. The initial casualties would be the husband and/or rapist killed by his wife/victim. The women would all say the same thing in their defense: "He had it coming."

The idea was that as long as there was one woman on the jury, no woman would ever be convicted for killing a man who had tried to force himself inside her. However, there were problems. For one thing, not all women were members of the church. Some of them thought that if a woman poisoned her husband's coffee, she deserved to do some time. Another problem was that the #1 cause of women killing their husbands was insurance. It often had nothing to do with abuse. (Other than the normal abuse of having to live with a man.) It was all about getting that big settlement and starting to date again.

At one point Celeste was inspired to try a real-life version of Aristophanes' "Lysistrata" and had all the members of her church withhold sex from their men until the church's demands were met. This was a disaster. It caused widespread defections to the church led by Chloe, whose attitude was: "whenever you get horny, have sex with your husband (or anybody else who's around)."

Celeste finally realized she needed a leader who was as charismatic as Cathy had been beautiful. At that time, Chloe was still saying things like: "The only good witch is one which a house has landed on." She was coming around, though. She recently told her audience:

"When you are being raped, call the cops and pray to Jesus. See who gets there first. Chances are you're going to die before you see either one."

Celeste felt she could work with Chloe as her High Priestess, but she had to get permission from either the stepmom or the couple that seemed to be raising her. The couple, Irene and Aggie were devout Buddhists. (At least, Irene was. Aggie was whatever Irene wanted her to be.) The stepmom and Chloe didn't seem to like each other much. Celeste didn't know what the story was there, and she didn't care. She decided she would approach Chloe through Starr. Maybe the stepmom wouldn't care what the kid did.

Aggie stuck her head in the door and asked, "What do you want me to do with Bonnie?"

"Who's Bonnie?" I asked.

"The girl I called you about. The one I found living in an underpass on I35, the one who refuses to go home. The one who says she'll kill herself before she goes near her stepfather, again."

"Oh, *that* Bonnie. Bring her in my office."

The little ball of filth threw herself on my couch before I could stop her. OH, well. That's why I buy flea powder by the case.

"Hey, honey. I hear you don't want to go home. What's the problem?"

"You sound like a kindergarten teacher on her first day," the fourteen-year-old said to me. "The *problem* is that the drug-dealing bastard that married my mom likes raping me more than he likes fucking her; and she likes heroin more than she likes me (or anything)."

"You know you wouldn't be the first kid to come in here and make up a bunch of shit about their parents…"

I liked the way her eyes flashed, and her nostrils flared. I felt like if I continued to insinuate that she was lying, I was going to have a fight on my hands. Good. A fighter has a chance.

"Don't worry, kid. No one will ever send you back to that kind of environment. Unfortunately, our options are limited. We are supposed to hand you over to the State of Texas. They will assign you to whatever state orphanage has room for you. From there, you will go to whatever foster parents choose to accept you. That is the only legal option the State offers us."

I watched the second-hand on the clock on my wall make a complete rotation.

"What's that, Bonnie? You want to know what other, perhaps 'not so legal' options there might be?"

"Oh, yeah. That thing. Right."

"Well, Bonnie. It just so happens that right behind us here on this hill is an orphanage that is not actually licensed by the State. Its school, <u>The Third-Eye Academy</u> is not accredited by the State of Texas, mainly due to the fact that its ethical teachings are based on Buddhism.

The school itself is run by Eirene and Aggie.

It's right up the hill, behind the hotel. Go check it out. You might make some friends."

"Are the arrest warrants ready?"

"I have prepared an arrest warrant to be served to Alys Loxley for eleven counts of obstruction of justice."

"Goddamn, Virgil, the charge is supposed to be kidnapping! Sappho Security was ordered to return those runaways to their homes. By refusing to do so, they are committing kidnapping. They are keeping those kids in that damn orphanage and brainwashing them. They are going to turn them into little commies."

"I'm telling you, Stanley, Kidnapping charges will never hold up in court. Not one of those kids will testify that they were coerced into staying at the Orphanage. They all love it, there. If we put them on the stand, they will testify that they fear going home. That's the reason I made the charges against Alys 'Obstruction of Justice'.

"No, I want the kids arrested and Alys charged with their kidnappings. That damn woman has been flaunting the law since she was in high school. I'm going to teach her a lesson: She and her 'lesbian liberals' are not above the law.

Virgil had his own reason for being aggrieved with Alys. She still had the shirt with his blood on it. She wore it every time she protested at City Hall. He would not mind putting Alys behind bars, but he didn't want to get beat up in court the way he had been beaten up in Alys's bedroom.

"Starr, that was great. I've never felt so relaxed and comfortable. Thank you."

"Just wait until we have sex."

"What the hell was that we just did?"

"Alys would call that foreplay."

"You wouldn't have her number, would you?"

"Lucky!"

"But, seriously, Starr. I've always hated that my mother named me Lucky, but tonight I feel it's the perfect name for me. The night that you and the grouchy lady came into my shop was the luckiest day of my life."

"Did you even know who that grouchy lady was?"

"No, but she was so good-looking, I assumed she was a model or a famous movie star."

"She is a State Senator, and, for a time, I was her personal assistant."

"You worked for her? What exactly does a 'personal assistant do?"

"Oh, you know. Arrange her schedule, screen her calls, fetch coffee; whatever is required."

"Whatever?"

Starr would not look her young protégée in the eye.

"Starr? You don't… Oh, my God."

"Oh, grow up, Lucky. It's that kind of a job."

In the weeks that followed, Starr did her best to make Cathy jealous by flaunting her thing with Lucky. They would party all night and Starr would tell the paparazzi that Lucky was "her own personal gypsy fortune-teller".

One Monday morning, Starr brought Lucky to work with her. Once they were inside the building, Starr kissed Lucky on the cheek and told her, "Babe, why don't you go upstairs and look around? I really do have an actual job to do, but we'll try to get together for lunch."

Upstairs, Cathy was in a funk. The residence she'd taken when she became a Senator was just palatial enough to remind her that she had failed in her royal ambitions. The three-story edifice stood on a cliff, overlooking the Colorado River, in Austin. As she stood on the balcony looking down on rafters and inner tubes, she thought about her past and her future.

"I was happier when I was delusional," she thought, "Catherine never had a moment of doubt about her right to call herself Queen. She was the daughter of Ferdinand and Isabella, royalty from conception. Even hungry and cold at Kimbolton, she never suffered the self-doubt that I am going through."

Cathy decided she needed some time alone. She got up and left her ladies scrabbling around and clucking like a gaggle of geese. She decided to go up to the virtually unused third floor. It was here, when they had first arrived that Starr had chased her, dressed like a pirate, and threatened to ravage her.

Cathy had long since forbidden such improprieties. "We must present a dignified front for the commoners," she told Starr, "it's a matter of 'Noblesse Oblige'." She knew that kind of thing was partly responsible for their recent estrangement, but she couldn't help it. The sad fact was that she cared about appearances and Starr didn't.

At the top of the stairs, Cathy came across a strange creature sitting on a bench. She was dressed in black and had a Tarot deck in her hand. Cathy did not recognize the medium she and Starr had visited months before. Cathy found the girl quite attractive in an elfin sort of way. She was astounded when the creature dropped to her knees and said, "Your Majesty."

Cathy sat on the bench the girl had just vacated and indicated that she should join her. "Who are you?" she asked the mysterious waif.

"My name is Lucky, Madam, but Starr said I should call myself 'Madam Aurora.'

"Oh, I see. You're Starr's little plaything," Cathy said. She was surprised by the pang of disappointment she felt. She stood up to leave.

"May I speak, Your Highness?"

The girl had prostrated herself at Cathy's feet. She looked up, adoringly. Cathy regally indicated that she could speak.

"It's true, Your Majesty. I am, indeed, 'Starr's little plaything'; but I am also clairvoyant. I can see that you are the reincarnation of, at least, three exceptional Queens. You, Madam, are the culmination of 1000 years of selective breeding. The world has been waiting for you, My Lady.

"Exactly which three Queens?"

"I think you are testing me, my Queen, and though I know you already know, I will answer. "In your soul, I clearly see the wraiths of Catherine de Medici, Catherine of Aragon, and Catherine the Great. I do not say, by any means, that they are the only noble souls who make up the Godlike Majesty that stands before me. They are merely the ones who shine the brightest. YOU, Your Majesty, are the long-awaited LILITH! Savior of Womankind."

"But, will I be Queen of something?"

The great poet, Bob Dylan said, "You don't need a weatherman to see which the wind is blowing."

Lucky didn't need a fortune-teller to know that Starr would use her and abandon her. She wasn't ready to go back to her "Reader" shack in Haltom City. That was OK. Lucky Betts knew how to cover all the angles. She intended to make herself indispensable to the Senator.

She was afraid she may have laid it on too thick with all the 'Lilith' bullshit, but Cathy had eaten it up. As long as she kept flattering the would-be Queen, she could ingratiate her way into the High Life. She would suck up to the Senator (literally, if necessary) until she was the official Astrologer of Senator Anderson.

Lucky felt kind of sorry for Cathy Anderson. She had obviously been over-indulged as a child. She had been given everything she ever desired, and the belief that she could attain Royalty was quite real in her. To use her delusions against her was another form of asymmetrical warfare. It was what she had called, when she was known as Evie, as "topping from below".

CHAPTER FOUR

Dawn Hightower sat in her Criminology class with her legs crossed like a man: right ankle atop left knee. Her posture, as well as her baggy pants and mannish button-down shirt were a sort of rebellion against her fiancé.

George Colter was a fireman on the North Side. He couldn't see his fiancée at this moment, but, if he could, he would not approve. He tried to make her as feminine as he could. "I like the shorter skirt," he would say, or "A little cleavage wouldn't hurt."

Dawn knew he was secretly ashamed of her. She knew he had "settled". She once heard the tail-end of a conversation that ended abruptly when she walked in: "…the best I'm ever likely to do." She didn't care. She had chosen to make her family happy and 'go straight'.

As the instructor droned on, Dawn began to get sleepy. Her roommate, Fiona, and Fiona's girlfriend, Daphne, had kept Dawn awake with their frolics in the next room the night before. Dawn dozed off and found herself (full of anticipation), unlocking the door to an apartment.

No sooner was she inside, than Alys was all over her, covering her face with kisses and whispering in her ear, "Get out of that uniform immediately, Nan. It's a bullseye for the bad guys." Then she ran and squatted behind the couch, pointing her finger and going, "Psew, psew,psew," like an eight year-old playing 'guns'.

Then, dreamlike, she was sitting in a hardback chair in the same position she sat in Criminology class. Suddenly, Alys grabbed her shoulder and fell to the floor.

"Sir, I'm hit," Alys cried out, dramatically. She crawled over to where Dawn sat with her legs crossed, ankle to knee. She rose up inside the triangle of Dawn's legs. She faced the vertex where Dawn's legs came together.

"Oh, my God, Captain! You've been hit, too. They got you with a poison dart. I'm going to have to get the venom out!"

"Alys Loxley, don't you dare! You are NOT peeing on me!"

Alys laughed until tears were rolling down her cheeks.

"You idiot! That's for a jellyfish sting. EW! NO, NO! I'm afraid I'm going to have to suck the venom out myself. In the line of duty, of course."

"Do what you must, Sarge. I'll try to take it like a man."

Dawn saw them both falling to the floor in laughter. She saw Alys looking at her with adoring eyes and saying, "I truly love you, Nan. Do you love me?"

Then Dawn was awake in Criminology class.

"Thank you, Dawn," the instructor was saying as he gathered his stuff and left the room.

"Why is the instructor thanking me?" Dawn asked the girl next to her.

"He asked if anyone had time to do an extracurricular investigation into the disappearance of the cheerleader. You yelled out, 'YES!'"

I knew Starr was an FBI agent. What I didn't know was that she was what is called a 'specialist'. That was the FBI euphemism for 'assassin'. She had lost an earlobe (and almost her life) in her last shootout which had bagged her the third "Top Ten Most Wanted" notch on her gun.

As a sort of 'Rest and Recovery' assignment, she'd been asked to look in on the disappearance of the TCU cheerleader. She called me and asked me if I wanted to go with her to interview the State Senator in whose district TCU was located.

"Why would I want to do that?" I asked.

"Her name is Cathy Anderson."

"I used to dream of the three of us being a sandwich," I told Starr, as we waited to led into the Senator's office.
"What?"
"Yeah, you and Cathy were the bread, and I was the bologna."
"Shut up, you idiot."

Despite Starr's attempt to put a damper on the day, I was pretty stoked when Cathy welcomed us without rising from behind her huge desk. I opened my mouth, but, before I could say anything, Cathy held her hand up, palm out, and said, "If you even think about saying, 'The gang's all here', I'll have you arrested."
"Fucking A," Starr agreed.
"Y'all are just mean," I mumbled.
Starr opened up a folder and began to read:
"Lily Inouye is a scholarship student from Manhattan Island, New York. She hasn't been to class in two weeks. She disappeared from her home in New York the same day her father was murdered in the same location. It's obvious that the suspect…"
"Missing person," Cathy interrupted.
"Oh, for crying out loud."
"Lily Inouye is not suspected of committing any crimes in the state of Texas, Special Agent Williams," Cathy snapped.
"Surely you don't think anyone else is responsible for the father's death?"
"Don't call her Shirley," I interjected, for a little levity. This resulted in cold, hard, humorless stares from both of them.
"A witness says he dropped Lily off at her house at ten after ten. That's ten to twenty minutes before the T.O.D." Starr read.
"Her mother says she sent her packing four hours earlier, when she found out Lily was gay. She says Lily was long gone before her husband arrived."
My mind was beginning to wander. I began to imagine myself in between Cathy and Starr, naked, on a bed.

"What about the neighbor that saw two women leaving the address at the time of the murder?" Starr asked.

I could see my tongue caressing Cathy's mound, a scene that had occurred countless times in the summer of '87.

"That description was vague. It could have been any two women walking down the block," Cathy insisted.

I could see Starr scissoring me in a frenzied passion, another image I had witnessed countless times.

Exasperated, Starr read the description: "I may have seen the blonde on TV before, but I didn't know the Hawaiian-looking one."

When I peek up from my ministrations on Cathy, I see the two of them fall into each other's arms and kiss passionately on the lips.

"'the Hawaiian-looking one', that sounds 'vague' to you?"

With one hand pushing my head down deeper into her lap, Cathy raises her other hand in the air.

"Does the FBI use 'racial-profiling, Agent Williams?"

Starr uses one hand to stick two fingers deep into me and raises the other hand to meet Cathy's in a big, ol' "High Five". I'M THE BASE OF AN EIFFEL TOWER! I've always dreamed of this!

"Well?" Cathy repeats, "What do you think?"

"YOU GUYS ARE FANTASTIC!"

When Chloe ran away as a child, she always ended up with Irene and Aggie. They were the nicest couple in the world. They always had time for her, and they didn't treat her like a dumb kid.

Unfortunately, today they were locked away in their bedroom when she got to the orphanage. They were making the kinds of noises which meant they were "making love". She knew she was on her own for an hour or so. She decided to walk around the campus and enjoy the view of the lake. The orphanage and school were built on a flat ridge that circled the hill. Halfway around the hill, she found a girl sunbathing on a towel. She was completely naked. She was sitting up alertly, sniffing the air.

"You're Chloe," she said.

"How do you know?"

"Because you smell like her."

Chloe decided to ignore this curious circular reasoning, and said, "Hi, Connie."

"Have we met?"

"No, but I've heard a lot about you on campus. You are quite the mysterious figure. Everybody here knows you're the Yoga instructor, but no one can remember when you got here."

"So?"

"So, some of these people have been here years. How can you have been here all that time and look my age?"

Connie mumbled something about 'dog years.' Then she dug some dirt out from under her towel for greater comfort. Some of it may have landed on Chloe.

Chloe decided to continue her walk around the hill. If she kicked a little dirt on Connie as she went by, it probably wasn't entirely intentional.

In a noticeably short time, Chloe had circled the hill and was headed back to the orphanage. She struck up a conversation with a new girl, Bonnie.

"How do you like it so far?" she asked.

"Frankly, it seems too good to be true. I've been here all day, and no one's told me to do anything. I haven't had to wash a dish, or dig a ditch, or clean a room, or fuck anybody. What's the catch?"

"It depends on if you want to stay or go. Have you ever heard that song by the Clash, "Should I Stay, or Should I Go?"

"I'm not familiar with it."

"Well, maybe it hasn't been written, yet, in this universe. The point is, if you're happy to go back to your parents or some random foster home, you can do whatever you want while you're here. But, if you're like most of these kids; you will gladly sweep, dust, or clean anything to stay.

As for the other thing, it doesn't happen here. The adults love the kids here. They are, literally, breaking the law to keep some of them safe. Ten that I know of, for sure."

"I think I'm the eleventh," Bonnie said.

"You're welcome," Stanley Scovall told the strung-out woman with the dried-up vomit on her shirt. "Go ahead and keep the bottle. Remember, whenever you have a problem, you can rely on your Mayor, Stanley Scovall, to help you. In the meantime, remember to be in my office at 8:00 sharp to sign that complaint. Don't worry about a thing. That "public drunkenness" charge will go away as soon as the papers are signed. When we are done, the judge will rule that Alys Loxley did, knowingly, refuse to return your daughter to her rightful mother, Sue Bairnes."

The woman struggled to focus on the Mayor. "Sue Bairnes, that's MY name!"

"Yes, very good, Sue. And we're going to get your daughter, Bonnie, back to you."

"Bonnie? Where is she? Is she alright?"

"Don't worry. We're going to get her back into your care, where she belongs, Sue."

"Sue? That's MY name, too!"

It always fell to Scout to retrieve the runaway, Chloe. Scout watched her play with the other kids. Watching her, Scout could imagine she was looking at a normal kid, rather than one with a pathological hatred of her stepmother. Scout knew that Chloe enjoyed listening to the kids who were as fucked up as she was:

"Daddy's an addict."

"Daddy beats us."

"Mommy's boyfriend touches me."

She would stand in front of them with a straight face and swear:

"The lady who calls herself my mom tore my real mom open and stole me out of her!"

Stanley made a check next to the name 'Bonnie Bairnes'. This made a total of eleven checks.

"I have eleven judicial orders for the return of the eleven runaways at Worthinghampton Orphanage," he said, "We will hit the orphanage at dawn. While the kids at the orphanage are being arrested, I'll be at Sappho Security Services making a very public arrest of Alys Loxley. I'm going to put an end to this Public Enemy #1, who turned my Cathy into a raging homosexual."

Virgil shivered, and noted that Stanley's laugh sounded a lot like Boris Karloff's.

"Sir, just to set the record straight; Alys always told me you hired her to seduce Cathy."

"WELL, SHE WASN'T SUPPOSED TO LIKE IT!"

Connie lay on the floor by the entrance to the orphanage. She growled when the phone rang. She picked it up and said, "Worthinghampton Orphanage, Constance speaking. How may I help you?"

"Hello. My name is Bonnie. I don't know if you know me. Today was my first day at the school. I have important news. There is to be a raid at dawn. The Storm troopers plan on grabbing the illegal runaways. They are also going to arrest Alys Loxley."

Connie dropped the phone and scrambled out the door, barking orders.

Bonnie looked down at the bound and gagged Virgil Wilder. "It's a good thing I decided to sneak a visit to my poor, old mom tonight. I heard you plotting with that crazy old man. I've got some good news and some bad news for you, Sancho Panza: The bad news is I'm going to have to keep you tied up until tomorrow. The good news is you're not going to be #1 on my death list."

A platoon of Texas State Troopers hit the Worthinghampton Orphanage at dawn. The flak jacketed, heavily armed men poured into the compound and were met with resistance in the form of women and children armed with cell phones.

Images of armored troops trampling innocent civilians (who were intentionally getting in their way) began to spread across the internet. Chloe ran as hard as she could into the side of a soldier, slapping a packet of McDonald's ketchup against her forehead. Then she staggered around saying, "Mom! Mom, where are you? Why aren't you here to help me?"

An hour later, they left. Not one of the eleven children on the list had been found.

District Attorney Stanley Scovall stood in front of the Worthinghampton Hilton, where Sappho Security was located. As he began to speak, cameras caught two burly troopers dragging Alys Loxley from the building. Her panties were down around her ankles. It was obvious to onlookers that the brutes had arrested her while she was on the toilet and hadn't even let her get decent. (In fact, a female trooper had repeatedly tried to pull the panties up, but Alys resisted and kept pulling them down.) Unwisely, Stanley continued his speech.

"Ladies and Gentlemen, Alys Loxley is a left-wing communist agitator from New York City. She has come down here to indoctrinate your children in the godless ways of Communism. She is taking children from their loving parents and enslaving them in schools where they are being brain-washed. Alys Loxley is telling your children that the Bible is not true. She is teaching them the devil-worshipping idolatry of "Lilith". When I try to unite these poor children with their God-fearing parents, she HIDES them from me!

Ladies and Gentlemen, Alys Loxley is not only a communist and an idolater; she is a HOMOSEXUAL! She wants to teach your children the deviant ways of Lesbos. Don't fear, folks. I'm not going to let that happen. I'm placing Alys under arrest for eleven counts of 'Obstruction of Justice'. Thanks to me, the streets of Fort Worth are safe again."

The two troopers put Alys in the back of a van that said <u>City of Fort Worth</u> on it. They hadn't even got the back doors shut before the van screeched away from the curb and went careening through the streets of Fort Worth.

Bonnie stuck her head out of the driver's side door and yelled, "Pussy Power!" Connie stuck her head out the passenger side window and went, "A-OOOOOOOOOOOOOOOOOOOO."

CHAPTER FIVE

The Cold War Heats Up

Nobody had any idea where Alys had escaped to. Sappho Security Services claimed they had no idea. Virgil had also lost all track of the eleven runaways he was supposed to arrest. Irene and Aggie said they knew nothing about it.

What little remained of Worthinghampton Orphanage was strictly legit. The instructors were all qualified teachers in the State of Texas. The orphans were all legal wards of the state. The food in the school kitchen was healthier than most public schools. The campus was cleaner and safer than any other school in Tarrant County. There was no legal way Scovall's goons could attack Alys's favorite project. So, they resorted to illegal means.

Manny Wasserman's mother had left him at a fire station a couple of days after he was born. The firemen tried to be charitable and say it wasn't her fault she left him, instead of on the doorstep, in a dumpster out back. "She may not have known any better," they rationalized, "with all the drugs in her."

When Manny had been weaned from heroin, he had been placed in a foster home. If he had been luckier, he might have been sent somewhere like Worthinghampton Orphanage where his psychosis would have been recognized and treated. Instead, he was passed from foster home to foster home where he learned to obey or be beaten. He was told that this Orphanage was run by lesbians who taught the children to worship the female demon, Lilith. He was told that the school regularly offered ritualistic sacrifices to the evil goddess. It was said that these sacrifices were often human. Manny didn't buy it; he was dumb, but he knew a porch from a dumpster.

Mo started following Manny around when they were eight. Eight years later, Mo was still following Manny around, doing whatever he was told. Mo knew how to say one word only: "Homer".

Jake hated all women, but one in particular. He hated Alys Loxley because he was convinced she was responsible for the death of his biological father, Joe Scarvino. He was well aware that the FBI hit-person, Starr Williams, was the one who had actually killed Joe Scarvino, but he blamed Alys. It was Alys Joe was trying to kill when Starr shot him. So, he hated her (though he'd never cared much for Joe).

Jake's stepdaddy had taught him how to make pipe bombs. He and Manny made half-a-dozen of them on that fateful Halloween night. Mo's job was to carry them up the hill.

"You got it, Mo?" Jake asked as he placed the 6th big old heavy pipe bomb in Mo's already trembling arms.

"Homer," Mo replied.

"Good boy, Mo. Well done."

Manny went on up ahead to scout for any trouble. It seemed quiet on the hill except a coyote baying from somewhere higher on the crags above. Manny made it to the entrance to the orphanage without seeing anybody. He lit a cigarette as he waited for Mo and Jake to catch up to him. The longer he waited, the more nervous that damned coyote made him. When Mo and Jake got there, he told them,

"Y'all spread them pipe bombs around the campus. Make sure you put some in the library and the cafeteria and the admissions office. Stay away from the dorms. We don't want to kill anybody, tonight. ("Except that damn coyote," he thought to himself.) As they went around planting pipe bombs with thirty-minute timers on them; he went on up the hill.

He walked about two hundred paces that took him around to the other side of the hill. He couldn't believe it when he saw a naked girl with a hairy bush, peering down the hill and listening intently.

Manny had given up on breaking into the library and was just taking the bombs from a wheezing Mo and setting them on the outside of the building. He was reaching for the third bomb when suddenly every light on the orphanage campus came on and a dozen loudspeakers began blaring Jerry Jeff Walker singing <u>Up Against the Wall, Redneck Mother.</u>

Bonnie Bairnes walked up to them with a baseball bat on her shoulders and said, "Howdy, boys!" Mo screamed "HOMER" and took a step back. He tripped on a step and fell. Pipe bombs went flying everywhere. One of the timers was activated. "29:59" it said. Then "29:58", "29:57".

The naked girl got excited when the loud music started playing. She jumped up and down and started clapping her hands. Then she raised her head up and started sniffing. Then she turned and looked right at him.

"Good-bye, Coyote," he said and shot her in the head.

The crazy girl with the bat blocked his escape down the hill so Manny ran upwards. Mo shouted, "HOMER" and followed him. The girl sauntered after them saying, "See you at the top."

A minute later there was a shot, and everyone froze. Mo cried, "Homer, Homer" and fell to the ground and covered his head with his arms. Jake and Bonnie began to run. As she passed the cowering figure on the ground, she said, "Hey, Dude!" Mo moved his arms and raised his head to see who was addressing him. Bonnie gave him a good thump on the head with her bat; just enough to hold him until she could come back.

Manny had never been able to hit a target. From the free-throw line, he would either pooch it halfway to the net or send it flying over the basketball backboard. He was having the same problem now, trying to rape a dead girl. He was pretty certain he had found the hole, but he kept missing the target. The harder he tried the softer he got. He was just about to go totally ballistic when he got the scare of his life. Apparently, he couldn't even shoot a bullet straight at the distance of ten feet.

His bullet had only scratched the girl's skull. She was still alive! She growled at him and hit him with a rock.

Jake and Bonnie rounded the curve of the hill at the same time. They saw Manny stagger to his feet, his head bloody, but still holding the gun. He pointed it their way and said, "Stop right there."

Jake sneered and began to unbuckle his pants. "Having a little trouble there, Manny? Let me show you how to do it. Keep your gun on this one here. Shoot her if she moves."

Connie tried to scramble to her feet, but Jake jumped her and knocked her back down. He savagely threw her over on her hands and knees. "Ya want to rape a girl right, you gotta do like this… Doggy Style!

With an evil laugh, he began to penetrate the helpless girl.

Suddenly there were a series of six explosions, one after the other. Rocks and debris fell everywhere. The entire hill was shaking. Bonnie rushed forward and took the gun from Manny's hand. She pressed the barrel between Jake's eyes and pulled the trigger.

Jake lay dead. Bonnie had taken her first life and the first battle in the War between Men and Women was over. World War Three had begun.

CHAPTER SIX

Through a Glass, Darkly

Lawrence Worthinghampton owned a 300,000-acre deer lease called "White-Tail Ranch". There was a tiny shack where a groundskeeper and his wife had lived years before, where Mr. W said I could lay low.

The fact is that what I was doing at the orphanage was illegal. The only recourse the orphanage had when we tracked down runaways was to put the kids in foster homes or send them back to their parents. Keeping them there where they could play with kids their own age in a loving and supportive environment was not a legal option.

Once you are past Dallas, the billboards on Eastbound I 20 start telling you all the fun you are going to have at White-Tail Ranch. Killing a bunch of large mammals is the main attraction, of course, but there is SO MUCH MORE! At the entrance is the wonderful "19th Hole". The first hole is off to your right when you drive in and the eighteenth is to your left. There is a large casino with three separate bars. There is lodging upstairs which, with the deluxe package, comes with female companionship. If you are unfortunate enough to have to bring your family with you, no problem; right off I 20, about a mile south on FM 26, on the east side of White-Tail Ranch is the <u>Dickinson Dude Ranch.</u> Wives and kids can enjoy a real wild-west experience (and hours of shopping) while hubbies are killing deer with high-powered rifles.

Bonnie and Connie dropped me off at my secluded cabin. They told me they had to get back to Ft. Worth because there had been a development. Bonnie told me what had happened:

"Aggie says that the news was like a constant replay of the poor defenseless kid, Chloe, wandering, dazed; blood (actually ketchup) all over her saying, "Mommy? Mommy, where are you. I need you, mommy.""

"Starr was freaking out," Irene added, "She said, 'I want Scout beheaded and her head displayed on a Pike. Why is Chloe running around in the middle of a battlefield, unsupervised? Do you realize what a bad mother that makes me look like?"

"She was still carrying on like the Queen of Sheba and blathering about her image when Chloe and Scout arrived. Scout marched stoically into the room. Chloe hid behind her.

"You're Fired!" Starr screamed at Scout.

Scout, who had been up all-night planning and aiding in my escape, said nothing. Chloe, who had hated her stepmother for as long as she could remember, said, "If Scout goes, I go."

Starr started to give her the "mom" speech. You know it: "I'm your mom and do as I say..." but then something seemed to break inside her. She shocked the room by abruptly saying, "You're going, but not with Scout. You are to be the next High Priestess of the Dianic Wiccan Church of Lilith."

As they prepared to leave, Bonnie gave me a warning. "Watch yourself around the proprietor of the 19th Hole. She's a tough old cougar who's gone through more women than Wilt Chamberlain. Her name is Anne Baldwin.

You could have blown me over with a Judas Kiss when I heard that Anne Baldwin was here. I hadn't realized that she worked for Mr. W. She was his 'head' secretary. (Sorry for the crude heterosexual joke. I just get so hot, *in so many different ways,* when I think about her.)

She and I have a, let's say, *colorful* history. Anne is bi-sexual, by which I mean she'll fuck anything human. (I've never seen her interact with aliens, so, as far as I know, that's where she draws the line.) The only living, breathing human being she has ever rebuffed was Yours

Truly. You see, for reasons of her own, little Eirene had set out to seduce me when she was thirteen. She wore very short shorts and loose tops. At strategic moments, when we were alone, I would catch glimpses of her little nipples. I didn't want to look, but it was like trying NOT to look at a celebrity's crotch when she drunkenly exits a limo. (You know what I mean?)

Irene guilt-tripped me into thinking I was a pedophiliac monster. I swore off sex. For twelve long, agonizing days I was celibate. Then the sadistic little wench admitting she was just playing with me. We were at the Worthinghampton Hotel at the time, and I immediately ran to the sexiest woman around- Anne. I told her, "You are the sexiest broad in the State of Texas! Let's get a room and I'll show you Nirvana!"

She leaned over the reception desk where she was working, revealing her magnificent cleavage, and told me,

"I'm just not that into you."

This was back in the days when Starr had worked for Cathy as her personal assistant. I got a call from one of my poker buddies, Lucky Betts.

"Big news," Lucky told me, "Starr has moved out. She's left Cathy. She tried to get me to go with her."

"You turned her down? I thought you had a major crush on her."

"I told her, 'I don't know, Starr. I've got a good gig here. Not since Joan Quigley was astrologer to Nancy Reagan has a fortune teller had so much power. Besides, I'm just getting used to sleeping on 1000 ct. sheets."

"In the end, she was jealous," Lucky said.

"I hate it when you come back to bed smelling of her" she said to me. "I kiss you and I taste her." I had to tell her what she had told me when I discovered the duties of a 'Professional Assistant'.

"Grow up, Starr. It's that kind of job."

Bonnie and Connie sat on the ledge where Connie liked to sunbathe. Connie, as usual, was naked. Her nudity had no effect on Bonnie. If Bonnie ever thought about sex, it was with revulsion and anger. She

tried never to think of it. Instead, she thought about more pleasant things…like murdering her stepfather. She was surprised, though, how hairy Connie's bush was.

"Don't you worry someone will see you naked?"

"Naw. The tourists tend to look down at the lake. These guys (she used her thumb to point up the hill) are always looking inward."

"What guys?"

"You haven't heard about the monks? Oh, Bonnie! You have got to see this. Connie threw on some basic clothes and led Bonnie up the path to the caves that snaked through the apex of the hill. Connie led Bonnie to the entrance of a cave and pointed. Bonnie looked in and saw an area the size of a normal living room. On the inner wall there was a television. Sitting on the dirt floor were three monks. They leaned back against various rocks and watched TV. It was broadcasting a rerun of NCIS. Continuously. One of the monks reached for the beer in his cupholder on his rock, and said, "I'm feeling adventurous tonight. I may switch over to 'Law and Order'."

The smallest monk said, "Hush. There're playing the Pepsi commercial I love so much."

Bonnie and Connie crept away from the cave.

"They never come out," Connie said, "They've forgotten the world outside the cave exists. The TV is all they know of life."

After observing the monks in the cave for a while, Bonnie and Connie decided to return to the orphanage. Bonnie couldn't resist writing a sign that said **DO NOT FEED THE MONKS.**

They were walking down the path, when Connie suddenly stuck her nose up in the air and began sniffing loudly. She signaled for Bonnie to get down. They hid behind a rock and watched as lines of Fort Worth police and State Troopers went by, beating the bushes, looking for runaways.

"Scovall's Storm Troopers," Bonnie said with disgust. Maybe I should put HIM on my list."

"What do you mean, Bonnie?"

"I'm going to kill a whole bunch of people. I'm making a list. I just haven't decided who my first victim will be."

"No, no, no. You mustn't ever kill, Bonnie. You may think I'm just a crazy bitch baying at the moon, but I've been given certain knowledge. I know that if you kill a human being, you will have to pay the karmic price eventually. If you kill, then either you or someone you love will have to die before their time. The only way to end a 'Life for a Life' spiral is to forgive. Can you forgive whoever inspired such murderous hatred in your heart?"

Bonnie thought about Eddy Skie. She thought about the first time she saw him standing over her bed. She thought about his first words to her: "Unzip me." She remembered the first fight. It was so unfair. He was big and strong. She was a thirteen-year-old girl. It hurt so bad. She was sure she would die. Then he told her again, "Unzip me."

Eventually, she did.

"No, Connie. I can't forgive him. I would kill him right now if I weren't so afraid of him. But one day, I swear; I'll add him to my list."

She thinks about it all the time. In her fantasy, she is just like Starr Williams. She is cool, calm, and cold-blooded. She holds the Walther PPK in Eddy's face. "Suck it," she tells him. He cries at first. Then, he realizes the helplessness of his situation, just as she did before. He knows there is no escape. He opens his mouth…

And she blows his fucking face off.

Scout still thought of Irene as a Buddhist monk. She knew that Irene and Aggie had gone all the way to Connecticut to get married, and since then, Eirene was simply Irene, but she was still drawn to Irene's serenity and peace.

"Will I ever see Lily again?" she asked her.

Irene took a long time to answer. Her first love had been her only love and that was how Irene thought it should be. However, her lifelong search for deeper spirituality (she was almost twenty-seven at the time) had told her that it wasn't always that simple. "There are different kinds of love," she began, as gently as she could…

Scout burst into tears.

Lily loved it when the Coven was rocking to the Merry Maiden's cover of Celebrate by Kool and the Gang. When Misty pulled her up on the stage and put a tambourine in her hand, she felt like she had gone to heaven. She was looking out at a room full of girls singing and dancing and drinking and laughing. They were all having a wonderful time and it was mostly because of the great music the band was making. And she was a part of that!

She was always disappointed when Robyn would say, "Thank you, folks," and they would quit for the night. After the first time she had 'performed' for the band, Robyn pulled her aside and said, "I'm sorry. I can't afford to pay you when you play for us." Lily laughed and said, "Trying to keep a beat with a tambourine and singing the few words I know is nothing to be paid for. It's the most fun I've had in my life."

"Our customers love you," Kate told her. "Our clientele has doubled since you joined us. Keep up the good work… and keep wearing those tight blue jeans."

One-night Lily donned her TCU cheer outfit and did the vocal lead on a rousing rendition of Girls Just Want to Have Fun. The crowd loved her. As she left the stage to deafening applause, it dawned on her:

"For the first time in my life, I'm having fun. I lived in fear most of my life, but now I'm free. THIS is what I've always wanted in life: to be free and have fun."

At that exact second, eight hundred miles away, Scout stopped listening to Irene and broke down into tears.

The more Chloe spoke about Lilith, the larger her audiences grew. Her show began to fill Will Roger's Auditorium twice a week. It was mostly women who came to hear her message. Women were tired of the patriarchy inherent in Christianity. New churches sprang up every day. The central tenet that divided the new "Lilitian" churches from the old Christian one was:

Did God make woman from the rib of Adam (thereby making women derivative and subservient?)

Before the fateful event of Jan 19, 2000, Lily had asked Scout to explain "The Blanchard Curse".

"My grandmother was a witch doctor in New Orleans. She was a very good witch doctor and a ruthless businesswoman. When a young woman named Ruby tried to set up shop in Grandma's neighborhood, Grandma set out to destroy her. Every magic spell that Ruby came up with, my Grandma would provide one that was twice as strong for half the price.

As a cruel joke, Grandma cast a spell on the neighborhood drunk that made him fall madly in love with Ruby. He followed her around like a love-struck schoolboy. He offered bouquets of weeds he had picked from the alleyway. He would serenade her in an off-key (but Loud) voice. He would pass out on her porch.

With no customers and an embarrassing beau, Ruby finally gave up. She left the neighborhood in disgrace, but not before putting a curse on Grandma.

"From now on," she swore, "Your eldest daughter and every eldest daughter after, will drive everyone she meets madly in love. They will be crazed with desire for her. Only if she returns their love, will it cease."

"That curse was the ruin of my mother, Kate Blanchard. She was a professor at TCU. A mad Irishman named Clancy fell for her hard. When mom got pregnant with me, she agreed to wed Clancy. By the time I was two, mom had decided that heterosexual relationships were not for her. She fell in love with a high school tennis instructor named Marjorie. When Clancy found out he got roaring drunk and came home yelling, "If I can't have you, no one will!"

I was frightened and ran to him, saying, "No, Dada, no." He back-handed me like an inside-low ball and I ended up bleeding profusely from my nose in foul territory. That was a mistake on the Irishman's part. Mom pulled out her revolver and shot him six times in the face.

Before she was sentenced to life in prison, she was asked if she felt any remorse.

"He had it coming," was all she said.

"You see the paradoxical predicament this presents," Lily said.

"If I return your love, it will set you free from the curse?"

"Exactly. What do you suggest?"

"Lead me on for about fifty years?"

"I like the way you think, Scout."

Now, after Lily's disappearance Scout worried about Lily's true feelings for her."

CHAPTER SEVEN

A Murder in Cowtown

Dawn Hightower looked down at the picture of the runaway TCU cheerleader and smiled at the irony. Just when she had given up on pursuing her secret yearnings and live a straight life, the mystery of Lily's disappearance had given her the perfect excuse to spend a lot of time in gay bars talking to beautiful women looking for other beautiful women.

Dawn ordered another beer and thought, "Sex with a man couldn't be that bad. Women do it every day. George Cotter is a good man. (Wait a minute. Is it 'Cotter' or 'Colter'? I'm not sure, but I'm pretty sure it's 'George'.)

When the waitress brought her beer, she asked, "You sheen this girl?"

"You asked me twenty minutes ago. The answer is still no."

"You're real cute, you know?"

"Really."

"Huh?"

"I'm not 'real' cute. I'm <u>really</u> cute."

"Well, I know, but you don't have to brag."

When the same girl brought her eighth beer and denied, for the third time, knowing Lily; Dawn told her, "You may not believe this, but I'm akshully gay."

"No shit," the girl responded, politely.

Dawn closed one eye, squinted, and pointed at the clock. "In half-an-hour I'm off-duty. In fact, I'm on vacation. I've got a great idea! I'm going to find Lily on my own time. Wanna come?"

"Why don't you give me your keys, hon.?"

After the last set on a Saturday night, it was definitely Party Time at the Coven. Misty had left at ten o'clock with a girl her own age, who claimed that with a combination of Yoga and Zen, she could maintain orgasm for an hour.

Lily met a lady called Philippa. Philippa told Lily she was a witch. "I'm a very powerful witch," she said with a wink. "I can fly on brooms and cast spells. I can turn you into a frog if I want."

"I used to be a frog," Lily replied, "I went to TCU. We were all frogs there."

They were both pretty hammered.

"Well, if you're already a frog, I'll turn you into a princess. I'll lock you away in a tower and put a spell on you."

"Will I have to spin straw into gold?"

"Not if you can make me say the magic word."

Lily kissed her.

"Um. Let's go to my place."

"Well, I was thinking more along the lines of "Rumpelstiltskin", but your place works."

Hecate Collins was a Fort Worth heiress, a cousin of the Basses, and a good friend of Starr Williams. She had no problem letting Starr crash at her downtown condo while Starr "got her shit together". Heck was watching a YouTube video of Chloe Dunnally-William's famous *End of Man* sermon from Texas Stadium in Irving, Texas. When Starr walked in, Heck immediately turned it off.

"That's OK," Starr said, "go ahead and watch my stepdaughter do her shtick. She craves attention." Starr's attention was drawn to a twelve-year-old bottle of scotch on the coffee table.

"Darling, it's 8:00 in the morning," Hecate pointed out.

"You're right," Starr conceded, "I'll get a beer."

While Starr enjoyed her first beer of the morning, Heck said, "I sense some hostility between you and your daughter."

"Stepdaughter."

"Yes, exactly. You know I would never do anything to upset you, dear."

"But?"

"Starr, I absolutely must have a franchise! That kid is the hottest investment opportunity since McDonalds. To be able to get a franchise now would be like investing in McDonalds before they sold their first million burgers. I'm thinking of putting a *Church of Lilith* where the old downtown library was. I could add branches as I went along."

"Hecate, Chloe's ego already (literally) fills stadiums. You're just encouraging her, for Christ Sake."

"Not for 'Christ's Sake, Starr. For Lilith's Sake! Jesus was a male. The men had their shot. For 2000 years, men have run with the ball…"

"A fucking sports metaphor? You have to be kidding me."

"Starr, I won't do it if you don't want me to…"

"No, no. Go ahead. But I warn you, the little brat is getting increasingly out of hand. Last week, she misquoted Voltaire, saying that "If there were no God, the Beatles would have had to invent one. The kid is shameless. People think she is the monkey, but she's the organ-grinder."

"And your point is?"

"I deserve a big, big cut."

"I've got my foot in the door, boss," Star Williams, formerly with the FBI, told her new boss, Lawrence Worthinghampton.

"Hecate is a legitimate, dues-paying member of the Western Association of Witches, Warlocks, And Wizards (or W.A.W.W.A.W.). She is not personally involved in any assassination plot, but she knows everybody! She's on the finance committee and anyone wanting funds for any kind of operation, must go through them. Don't worry. I'll get to the bottom of this."

Lily became obsessed with Philippa. She could not stop thinking of her. It wasn't just the sex, which was mind-blowing; it was the aura of mystery that surrounded Philippa.

Misty warned Lily that Philippa was a Master of the Dark Arts, but Lily didn't care. Philippa was cool, hip, sophisticated, and powerful. She was everything little Lily from Manhattan wasn't. Lily wanted to be with her all the time.

Philippa lived in a creepy house next to a cemetery. She lived with two other witches, Agatha, and Mildred. One night, after a meeting between the three witches, Philippa joined Lily in bed.

"I have some interesting new," she told Lily. "State Senator Anderson is vacationing at <u>Dickinson Dude Ranch</u> for two weeks this summer. Even more interesting is the fact that she has invited the little evangelist girl to go with her. I need you to go with me to Texas. Will you do that for me?"

"Of course, but how can I help?"

"I sense a great power in you, Lily. I think you could be one of the greatest witches of all times if you let me guide you. Will you do that, baby?"

"Yes, my love. I'll do whatever you want."

Lily soon learned that being a Witch's Apprentice meant doing the lion's share of the driving on a long trip. She was exhausted by the time they checked in to their downtown hotel in Fort Worth. Still, she didn't want to be separated from her lover and teacher. When Philippa announced that she had a meeting to go to, Lily begged to go along.

Philippa looked at the girl's innocent, expectant face. She sighed. It was a sad fact of life that a girl could never feel the heights of ecstasy until she had felt the pain of a broken hymen. With a sad smile, she said,

"OK. You need to learn about this side of witchcraft, as well. It's not all potions and riding brooms, you know."

They walked a few blocks to Hecate's place. They were greeted by Hecate and her roommate, Starr Williams. The four of them chatted for half-an-hour or so. Then, at some unspoken signal, Hecate followed Philippa into the bedroom.

Lily could not believe it. She stared at the bedroom door in shock. Less than 24 hours earlier she and Philippa had been in each other's arms. Their passion had been intense; their love undeniable. Now, listening to the unmistakable sounds of Philippa being pleasured; Lily realized it had meant nothing to Philippa. Silent tears ran down her cheeks.

"How 'bout dem Cowboys?" Starr tried, but it didn't lighten the mood. She tried another tack: "Would you like a drink?"

"It's 10:00 AM."

Philippa was making no effort to muzzle her pleasure.

"Maybe I will have that drink."

While mixing up a Mimosa, Starr asked, "Are you new to witchcraft?"

"I've been Philippa's disciple for a week."

"Well, if it's any comfort to you, what's going on in there has nothing to do with romance. In the world of witches, THAT is a ritual involving power and dominance."

"But they're FUCKING!"

"It's not like regular fucking. In fact, my roommate, Hecate, has no interest in sex with women. She's totally straight. Oh, she'll be bragging next week to other witches about what's going on in there right now. But she'll be bragging because of the proximity to power that she has achieved. Her witch friends, gay and straight, will be envious."

As she handed Lily her drink, she said, "Witches are not monogamous. If Philippa has singled you out you must have some hidden power."

"So she tells me."

"Search for it inside yourself," Starr told her. "You might want to find it before she does."

———— ❧ ————

After two weeks, Dawn realized she would never go back to her old life. Nine nights of cruising gay bars and talking to girls who were fun to be with had convinced her. <u>This</u> was the life she was destined for. It was not the life her family wanted for her. It was not the life her peers would approve of. It was HER life, damn it. No one would tell her how to live!

She was high AF.

When the blue-haired girl gave her that soulful kiss (with the LSD cap on her tongue), she knew she was not going back to the firefighting dick in Ft. Worth. She had a new purpose in life. She was going to find the mysterious girl named Lily. She knew that when she did, she would find the Meaning of Life. She realized it was her destiny to find the girl and it WOULD happen, no matter what.

"I don't even have to try," she realized, "I just have to accept the Will of the Universe."

Yes, she was seriously fucked-up; but the interesting thing was, at the very instant she stopped trying, she found her.

"She joined up with the 'Maidens', she did," the blue-haired girl said when they came up for air.

"The who?"

"No, not the "Tommy, Can You Hear Me?" chaps. "The Maidens."

"She's in a band?"

"'at's right. An all-girl band. Out of Seattle. Want to go my place and shag?"

But Dawn was staring out into space, rapt at the wonder of it all. This was the end of her old life; and the beginning of a brand new one. She could hear the words being spoken softly to her (She didn't realize she was listening to Emerson, Lake, and Palmer on the radio):

> "You see it's all clear,
> You were meant to be here…
> From the Beginning."

———— ❖ ————

Anne has gotten in the habit of coming to my little cabin on Mondays when business is slow. It's not a date or anything. It's just two girls discussing their weekends and having a few glasses of wine. The jaded sophisticate, Anne Baldwin will pretend indifference towards me…AS IF!

ME! The greatest explorer of the bush since Dr. Livingston! No lesbian or bi-sexual is "just not into me"! Not on my watch.

The sound of her jeep announces her imminent arrival. I am ready for her. I have squeezed into my tightest shorts, sans panties. I have a push-up bra to emphasize my lovely itty-bitty titties. (I once had humongous titties, but they were shot off. *See Book One.*) I have expensive perfume that I stole from Cathy. (She told me it smelled good on me.) My snakeskin boots are "East Texas Chic". I feel confident! The game is afoot!

She enters my humble cabin like a million-dollar model stepping out of a *Cosmo* shoot. She does the hair-toss. How does she manage to make it go in slow motion? She sniffs at the Rum and Coke I hand her. She doesn't touch it.

"Do you have anything besides rum?" she asks.

She knows I do. I hastily make her something with vodka in it and she deigns to accept it. I make sure my fingers do not brush hers.

"Did you show the boys a good time before they went out to slaughter deer," I asked, wittily.

"Did you masturbate after I called?" she replies.

My face is instantly red. I'm embarrassed, shocked, flustered, aghast, and very, very angry. This is beyond the pale. This is inexcusable. One does not ask such a thing!

The most galling thing is that it's true. I'm undecided whether to scratch her eyes out or throw myself at her feet and say, "Please take me," when she smiles and says, "Guess who checked in today?"

Well, I don't care, do I? I only want to melt this Ice Queen.

"Your old friend, Beatrice Inouye."

"What? Beatrice? Here?"

"Very eloquent rejoinder, dear. Lawrence has put her in the penthouse this weekend. He wanted me to tell you. I think he hopes the two of you will have a conversation."

I want to ask her what Worthinghampton wants me to find out from Beatrice. I want to ask her if he thinks Lily is involved in the plot against Chloe. But, mainly, I want to rip her clothes off and fuck her until she begs for more.

Instead, the cruel cunt-teaser makes her exit, leaving me alone... with my vibrator.

Philippa came alone the next day. Starr was glad she hadn't brought the kid along. Today, Philippa would have to show her cards and tell Hecate what she planned. If Hecate refused funding, Philippa might cut up rough, and Starr didn't want the kid to be upset any more than she was. She felt attracted to the girl. Lily reminded her of Alys; seemingly simple, but with hidden depths.

After a few minutes of general conversation, Hecate asked Starr to go get her a pack of cigarettes. "Take your time," Hecate told her. It was her posh way of telling the help, "Get lost for a bit while we discuss business." Starr didn't mind. With the unlimited resources her new boss could provide, she had wired Hecate's place six ways to Sunday and the receiver was in her purse. She went down to the coffee shop on floor level and listened in on the conversation above her.

When Hecate had first learned of the plot to assassinate the child prophet, she had scoffed. She had told the other members of WAW WAW:

"If we go around killing people, we are no better than men. This is a watershed moment in Human History (or 'Herstory', she added, wryly). The tide has turned. Men's era of rule is over. And who is spreading that word most effectively? The very one you propose to martyr."

The majority of the Council agreed, and the plan was shelved. Later, however, a secret cabal, led by Philippa and her roommates, Agatha, and Mildred, decided that a peaceful, evolutionary process would take too long. They wanted women in control NOW. They wanted war, and a martyr would assure that.

Sex with a powerful witch is like a lie-detector. Philippa now knew exactly where Hecate stood. It was with great regret that she took Hecate's head in her hands and broke her neck.

"You are absolutely correct," Philippa said, as she laid the corpse down on the floor. She continued to talk as she erased any evidence that she had ever been there. "We must proceed peacefully. In a hundred years or so, our numbers will be strong enough to take a stand."

Philippa took Starr's FBI issued weapon out of her purse as she said, "Excuse me, Hecate, I have to use the restroom. She stepped out into the hallway and called 9-1-1. "Hello, my name is Starr Williams. I discovered my friend planned to kill my stepdaughter, so I shot her. Her body is in Room 211.

No longer worried about the listening devices that she knew were in the room, she continued sending a location as she walked back into the room and shot Hecate between the eyes. She dropped Starr's gun and went downstairs on the elevator. As she passed the coffee shop, she smiled at the bewildered look on Starr's face.

The gun must have fired close to one of the bugs. The sudden **BOOM** almost burst Starr's eardrum. She hadn't expected it. Hecate and Philippa hadn't been arguing. Philippa had been droning on about cooperation or some such shit and Hecate had not even bothered to answer.

When she saw her gun, Starr knew she had been framed for murder. By the time the coroner discovered the broken neck, she would be the prime suspect. And the DA would not look very hard for another one. Resisting the urge to take her gun, Starr got out of there. The sirens were right outside. She called Lily as she exited the building.

"Your traveling companion is crazy and dangerous as fuck. Get away now. Go to the prearranged rendezvous."

CHAPTER EIGHT

CLOSE ENCOUNTERS

We met at the fancy restaurant of the '19ᵗʰ Hole'. Beatrice was only a month or so older than me, but the escorts hurrying to meet their Johns for dinner might have mistook her for my mother. Time had not been kind to Beatrice. She had obviously had a hard life.

"Beatrice! My, don't you look great!"

"You're Lily's new girlfriend, aren't you?"

"I haven't met Lily. I was once your girlfriend, though. Remember Marymount?"

"Alys?"

"I was madly in love with you, Beatrice. I gave you my heart and soul."

"I ain't gay."

"You may not be gay, but you were singing like a canary when my tongue was spelling out the alphabet on your clit. You were trilling like an operatic soprano by the time I got to "H"."

"You gave me the only orgasm I ever had in my life. Damn you!"

There was a brief moment when Beatrice's eyes seemed to clear.

"I was so afraid, Alys. My superstitious mind conjured all sorts of horrors that might happen if I acknowledged my feelings for you: ostracism, public censure, eternal damnation.

Now I see that nothing I could have imagined could have been worse than the reality I created for myself when I spurned your love. I have died a thousand cowardly deaths."

I had done my best to forget Lilith, but she forced herself into my consciousness here, and made me say to Beatrice, "Take heart, my love! You will get another chance. It may not be in this lifetime but be ready. Always be ready to grab love when you get the chance."

Beatrice took my hand and kissed it gratefully.

I hate sappy, emotional scenes like this, so I said to Bee, "Hon, a guy named 'Worthy-something-something' is picking up the tab for this meal, so I need to ask you, "Is there anything unusual you can think of about Lily or her dad, Jack Hardy?"

"Jack's not her father."

"What do you mean, 'Jack's not her father?' I was standing there less than a hundred yards away when she was conceived. Remember, you staggered out of the car and fell at my feet?"

"Oh, no. She wasn't conceived until hours later when the UFO beamed me up and the aliens abducted me."

Dawn walked into The Coven and sat at the bar.

"How may I help you?" Kate asked.

"I'm looking for a girl," Dawn replied.

"Let me rephrase that. What can I get you to drink?"

"Oh, I'm not thirsty, I just want to find this girl." Dawn held up a picture of Lily. "Have you seen her?"

"Get out."

"Hey, I'm not a cop. I don't even care whether she killed her father or not."

Kate took a baseball bat out from behind the bar. "I'm warning you," she said.

Dawn gabbed the bat, pulled the hefty bartender over the counter, and used the bat as a chokehold.

"I'm not going to hurt her. I just want to find the meaning of life."

Beatrice ordered her third whiskey. I was nursing a cranberry vodka.

"The commander of the aliens looked like Grace Parks. You know, the girl who played "Kono" on *Hawaii Five-O*. Commander Kono told me, 'The man who intercoursed (Sic) you left no seed. We will fill you with a *special* seed! Your child will be a Savior.

Somehow, I didn't think this was what Mr. Worthinghampton was looking for, but I couldn't find anything else about Lily that was unusual. (Sadly, having a violent, abusive dad was not that unusual.)

"And you maintain that Lily was nowhere around when Jack Hardy died?"

"No, like I told the kid from TCU, Lily…"

"Excuse me. What TCU kid?"

"She called herself 'Dawn'. Sweet kid, good with the jokes.

"Dawn Hightower?"

"Yes. I told her and I'll tell you. I threw Lily out of my house hours before Jack came home."

"Did Dawn say why she was asking questions about…? Let me ask you this. Did Dawn seem more interested in Lily's whereabouts than Jack's death?"

"That was all she wanted to know. Where did I think Lily went?"

Curiouser and curiouser.

Beatrice went back to her lonely life in Manhattan. I went back to my lonesome bungalow. I had come up with only one thing from Beatrice that might be of interest to Mr. Worthinghampton. I wrote what I knew in a secret code:

AwnDa IghtowerHa is an ooselA annoncA[3]

Lily sat on a comfortable bench outside the serpentarium at the Fort Worth Zoo. This was Starr's designated rendezvous point. She felt a little self-conscious in her dark sunglasses and large cap, but Starr's message had alarmed her. She knew Philippa was a powerful witch, but she wasn't sure just what powers she might have. She didn't know

---

[3] Dawn Hightower is a loose cannon

if Philippa could find her wherever she was, but she thought she should try to disguise herself as much as she could.

All the cloak and dagger stuff was fun, but, after an hour, Lily was getting bored. She decided to walk the short distance to the zoo restaurant and get a bite to eat.

Even in early May, the relief of the air-conditioning in the restaurant was appreciated. Lily ordered a turkey sandwich, figuring nobody could mess up a turkey sandwich. As she ate, she watched the ubiquitous sports event on the inevitable TV Screen. She almost choked on her (too dry) turkey sandwich when pictures of Starr and Hecate appeared in the corner of the screen and a banner ran across the bottom saying:

FORT WORTH SOCIALITE MURDERED IN HER DOWNTOWN APARTMENT. POLICE SEEK ROOMMATE FOR QUESTIONING.

Lily returned to the Texas heat and headed for the zoo exit. Starr couldn't show her face in a public place now. Lily needed a plan B. Her old dorm was less than a mile away, but she hadn't been back there in three months and that place might be watched. She was alone and afraid. It reminded her of times when she had hidden in the closet while her father was beating her mom. When he stormed out of the house, she would crawl out to her bleeding mother.

"If anything should ever happen to me, go to Alys Loxley. She loved me and she'll take care of you," her mom had told her. Lily knew that help could be reached at Sappho Security Services. She called a taxi to pick her up at the zoo. Still frightened, she made a stop at the Gift Shop on the way out; but when she got into the taxi the driver said, "Ma'am, I don't know what you're hiding from, but if you're going for incognito, you should lose the gorilla mask.

Cathy found Chloe swimming in the Olympic-size pool in Cathy's back yard. Irene and Aggie sat by the pool.

"Can we get down to business," Cathy asked, "or do we have to wait for the kid to finish playing?

"Chloe has final say on any deal, but she is not detail-oriented," Aggie explained. Irene and I can work out a deal we think she will agree to."

"OK. As I have said, I am kicking off my campaign for Governor of Texas this month. I would, quite frankly, like to associate my campaign with Chloe's message of Female Empowerment. I propose that I write a short memoir in which I detail the guiding force I've provided to Chloe in her religious upbringing. In her endorsement, Chloe could mention "the positive maternal influence" I've provided her as well as "the strong moral leadership".

Aggie started to give a polite answer, but Irene interrupted. "There will be no endorsement from Chloe."

"But why?"

"The unfortunate publicity lately concerning Chloe's stepmother has been bad enough, but now this." Irene showed Cathy the headline from the morning paper:

HER PERSONAL FORTUNETELLER CLAIMS SENATOR ANDERSON IS THE REINCARNATION OF LILITH.

"It's too much, Cathy. We need to keep Chloe away from all that. We can't have her seem to endorse anybody as the messiah."

"CHLOE," Cathy yelled, "Do you think I'm Lilith?"
Chloe laughed so hard; she blew water out her nose.
"I'm going to take that as a no," Cathy said.
Aggie pointed out, "She's such a contrarian, you just have to suggest the opposite of what you want her to say."
"You just have to know how to handle her," Irene said. "Watch this. Chloe, what's the difference between ignorance and indifference?"
"I don't know, and I don't care."

———— ❧ ————

Leaving the Coven, Dawn noticed a movement in the corner of her eye from behind a dumpster. The day was overcast with a slight mist, but Dawn was sure she had seen something. Her natural athletic instincts and her criminology training enabled her to spin around, grab the assailant, and lift her into the air in the blink of an eye. The third part of this single fluid motion was tossing the attacker into a brick wall. It was just then that Dawn's brain caught up to her reflexes and she realized she was about to smash a kid's head into a wall. She stopped, but the impetus landed them both in a puddle. They sat, tangled up together, while a light rain soaked them.

"I don't know why they call it a 'funny' bone," the girl complained, it hurts like fuck."

"Watch your language, young lady. What's your name, anyway?"

"It's Misty."

"Yeah, it sure is. My coat is soaked through, already."

"That's my name, dumbass. I'm Misty."

"Why are you following me, Misty?"

"I overheard you talking to Kate. Let me see the picture."

Kitty showed it to her.

"Yeah. That's Lily. Do you swear you're not a cop?"

"On the contrary. I had a vision. Me and the blue-haired girl saw her in a blaze of glory. I've given up my career, my family, my past, and my future. My entire purpose in life is to see her on an earthly throne.

"You're not in love with her, are you?"

"I worship her."

"That's fine. Worship her all you want; just remember she's mine."

"So, where is she?"

"She's running with some bad company. She got herself mixed up with a wicked witch named Philippa. Philippa is trouble, man. They're headed down the "Highway to Hell".

"And where does that highway lead?"

"Straight into Texas, of course."

CHAPTER NINE

You Say Hello, And I Say Goodbye

"Hello?"

"Hello, Scout, it's me, Lily."

"LILY! Oh, my god! Is it really you? I can't believe it. I'd almost given up hope. I feared you might be dead. Oh, thank god."

"No, Scout. Don't thank any deities or anything. I'm fine. I just wanted you to know you didn't have to worry about me anymore."

"Not worry about you? What kind of crazy talk is that? Of course, I worry about you, my love."

"Well, see, that's the thing. A lot has happened to me recently…"

"Oh, yes. It must have been horrible for you, my darling, being kidnapped by that 'Manson-like' gang."

"I don't know what you heard, Scout, but I assure you the girls I was with were very nice."

"Oh my god, I've heard of this. It's the 'Stockyard Syndrome'. They've turned you into Patty Hearst!"

"No, really. They were very nice. They let me play in the band. I was so happy. Then I made a terrible mistake."

"WHAT?"

"I fell for someone. I thought she was great. She seemed larger than life. She was my Idol. I adored her. Then, I found out she wasn't what she seemed. I discovered that she was really a terrible person who didn't deserve my love. Has this ever happened to you, Scout?"

CLICK

Connie shook Starr awake, gently. "You have a visitor."

Starr, wanted for questioning in the murder of Hecate Collins, was sleeping in a cave overlooking Lake Worth. She looked past Connie and saw Lucky.

"You may as well have brought the sheriff," Starr told Connie, "this one will sleep with the enemy if the 'thread-count' is high enough."

"Oh, get over it, Starr. No one made you leave. No one made you move in with Hecate and become involved in a murder."

"I'm on a job, Lucky. I'm investigating a potential assassination attempt."

"I thought you had quit the FBI."

"I did. I work for a higher power, now."

"God?"

"Almost. Lawrence Worthinghampton. His hand seems to be in everything and, right now, he's very interested in keeping my stepdaughter, Chloe, alive. It seems a splinter group of terrorist-witches want to give Chloe the gift of martyrdom. I'm hoping I can blow that up before it happens."

"Cathy is 100% behind you, Starr, but she can't interfere with a police investigation."

"So, she's 100% useless, as always. But she's still purty, ain't she?"

"We used to hear what the cops were up to from Dawn, but she's disappeared."

"Sounds suspicious."

"Cathy says Dawn is a responsible, down to earth, level-headed girl. She wouldn't do anything crazy."

"She fell in love with Alys Loxley."

"Yeah, well, there's a lot of that going around."

"Hey!"

"Just saying." Lucky looked around at the surroundings. "How long you going to be living in a freaking cave, girl?"

"Until I can come up with an alibi. Right now, the frame seems airtight. I was seen leaving the premises minutes after the murder, she was killed; no, scratch that, she was *shot* with my gun, and, if the police find my listening devices, they will hear Philippa apparently plotting with Hecate to murder my stepdaughter. It doesn't look good.

"Videotape! The condo has security cameras in the halls and elevators. They are time stamped. If we can get them, we might be able to prove you weren't there when she was killed. I'll get right on that. What are you going to do?"

"I'm going to try to find a young lady named Lily. I think she may be over her head in a witch war."

Lily was surprised to see a scraggly girl of about fifteen behind the receptionist's desk.

"Syphilitic Spermatozoid Supply," the grubby gamine said with a grin, "How may we fill your order?"

Lily heard a bark of laughter from under the desk. "I think I may be in the wrong place."

A beautiful woman who looked to be in her thirties, rushed in and said, "Bonnie, Connie, you girls get out of here, now. Get back over to the school."

The beautiful lady held out her hand. "Hello, I'm Martha. I'm sorry, I'm here alone right now and having to do all the work. Those chicas offered to help. I should have known better."

As Martha spoke, the girl Lily had talked to was cartwheeling out the door and another (equally dirty, but naked) one was scampering after her.

"*What an enormous bush,*" Lily couldn't help noticing.

"My name is Lily. I'm looking for Alys. My mom said she would help me."

"Lily. Your mom is Beatrice, right? I think I'm aware of your situation. "The authorities in New York want to talk to you concerning the events surrounding your father's death.."

Lily paled and Martha hurried to her side. She took the young lady's arm and said, "I'm sorry. That was tactless. Come on back to my office, and I'll make you some tea."

While Martha prepared the tea, Lily looked at the pictures in her office.

"I assume these gorgeous children are yours?" she asked.

"Yes. The handsome fellow is Tom Junior. He's nine, and the nina's are Dawn 7, Rosa 5, and Deborah 2."

"They are beautiful. *Muy Bonita.* Is that right?"

"Close enough. Listen, Lily. I'm afraid Alys is unavailable right now. I'm not supposed to reveal her whereabouts to anyone, but maybe I can help you."

"Oh, I hope so, Martha." Lily began to cry. "I've got myself in a terrible mess. I think I'm involved in a murder. Starr's disappeared. She says I'm in terrible danger from my ex-girlfriend, and I broke a really nice girl's heart. I don't know what to do!" She began to sob.

Martha comforted the poor child as best she could until Lily fell asleep. Then she called Alys.

"Honey, if I put a worried, sensitive young woman in that cabin with you, you wouldn't seduce her, would you? Alys? Hello?"

Dawn almost put Misty out of the car in Oregon when she discovered that the kid had no sense of humor. After staring off into space for minutes, she would say, "But *why* did the chicken want to get to the other side of the road?"

Getting the kid to talk about herself was downright depressing. The girl was seriously glad her mother was in rehab, so Misty didn't have to take care of her and could go on this adventure. She had been taking care of her mother as long as she could remember. All Dawn had to do to change to a less depressing subject was say the magic word: LILY.

"Lily is not a regular person," Misty would say, "She's different. She is surrounded by an otherworldly aura."

"You've seen it?"

"Yeah."

"Were you stoned?"

"Well, ye-a-ah." Misty rolled her eyes. "I don't mean she's 'angelic' or 'ghostly'. She's tough. She's got those biceps and shit, man. She's strong. When she held me, I felt safe. I wanted to have sex with her, but she wouldn't do anything but hold me and kiss me like I was her treasured doll. After Kate talked to her, she wouldn't even kiss me on the lips. She started acting like a mom. Can you imagine my frustration? To be so close to a beautiful, strong, passionate woman and be treated like a child? It was too freaky, too messed up. I started to avoid her. I started hanging out with Willow. Willow's alright. She's my age but she's about half-crazy. She goes around telling everyone her orgasms last an hour. YEA! Nice for her! She gets the hour-long orgasm. I'm the one with the worn-out tongue.

Anyway, Lily started hanging out with Philippa. She is bad news. Her girlfriends don't become exes, they just disappear. They either commit suicide or go back to Kansas. Either way, they're dead. I thought I was dead until she came along. I was just a kid, but Philippa made me feel like a sexy woman. She used me until she tired of me, then she gave me to her sisters. When they were through with me, they threw me away like a used condom. I nearly died of shame and grief.

Then Lily came along. She was being kidnapped by a bunch of strangers, but she still had the compassion to find out why I was so depressed. She held my hand and talked to me all that night in the van. She brought me back to life. And she made me a promise. Do you want to hear it? It's supposed to be a secret, but I think it'll be alright if I tell you."

"OK. Go ahead. Tell me what she promised you."

"She promised one day she would bring me Philippa's head as a present."

"I hope I'm there on that day," Dawn told her.

CHAPTER TEN

Take this Job and Shove it

"Senator Anderson's residence. How may we direct your call? Ever since Starr had left, Lucky had been forced to take over all the personal secretary chores, as well as her own astrological chores and she was not happy about it. Without bothering to cover the speaker of the phone with her hand, she yelled,

"Hey Cathy, it's for you."

Cathy came into the room pulling on a silk kimono. She had been sunbathing nude and watching the tourists rafting and inner tubing down the Colorado River. From Cathy's mansion on the top of the cliff, the revelers on the river looked like ants.

"Who is it," she asked.

"That guy with too many syllables in his name, Willoby or whatever."

"Ahh, Mr. Worthinghampton, how delightful to hear from you. I apologize for the rudeness of the staff. I've been forced to get rid of some of the help lately and you know what they say about 'good help'."

"That it comes in handy in times of need?"

"Oh. Well, yes. Quite. Indeed," Cathy stammered, slipping into an awful British accent.

She was so flustered that she aimed a playful kick at Lucky's rear. Lucky grabbed her foot and had Cathy hopping around until they both fell on the couch, laughing. Lucky began to tickle Cathy which caused her to drop the phone into the cushions and when they both dove for it, they bumped heads.

Cathy was still giggling when she resumed talking. "What can I do for you, sir?"

"Well, first of all you could try to cheer up."

"Sorry about that, sir."

"No, no. It pleases me that you are in such good spirits. Cathy, let me start by saying that I don't care about the personal lives of people I've helped to attain positions of power. They can do whatever they want as long as they tow the party line, you know: "rugged individualism", the "bootstrap" thing- I can't remember exactly how that goes, but you know what I mean."

"Yeah, I know the one you mean, although it's hard to figure how someone pulls themselves up by their bootstraps."

"Seems like they would fall over, doesn't it?"

In the tussle on the couch, Cathy's kimono had come loose, and Lucky's tickles had become caresses.

"Yes," Cathy answered. Then, when Lucky began to suck on her nipples, she added, "Yes, indeed."

"Ms. Anderson, allow me to lay my cards on the table. I need to find out as much as I can about Alys Loxley. I have been informed that, at one time, you and Ms. Loxley were close, *very* close."

Lucky was doing a thing with her fingers that made speech difficult for Cathy. "Mmm," was about all she could manage.

"Please don't get me wrong, Cathy. I don't mean to be salacious. It's just that I had a very definite idea about her character when I put her forward as the High Priestess of the Church of Lilith. However, since the assassination attempt, she's become quite unpredictable and a bit of a loose cannon. My sources tell me that she's become a true believer in spirituality and communicating with the dead, and such nonsense. I always thought she was a girl with her head screwed on tightly and her feet planted firmly on the ground.

To Cathy's horrified amazement, Lucky grabbed the phone out of her hand and began to berate Mr. Worthinghampton:

"Have you never lost someone you love, sir? It is not kooky to believe that the soul is immortal, nor is it stupid to want to reach out to one who has been ripped from your life as Nan was from Alys's. I have spoken to Alys about this, and I happen to know that she believes that a young girl by the name Dawn is the reincarnation of Nan Butler. If it gives her comfort in her grief to believe such a thing; what gives you the right to question how tightly her head is screwed on or how firmly her feet are planted?"

There was a full ten seconds of silence.

Then, Lawrence Worthinghampton said, "You are quite right, young lady. The scientific view of existence is a cold, comfortless view. It provides no comfort for lives tragically cut off in the prime. I shouldn't have even brought it up, but as long as I've got Cathy on the phone, there is one other thing I wished to speak to her about.

I don't know if you keep up with things European, Cathy, but Baron Von Parkesburg was recently my guest and he says his mother is insisting that he marry soon."

Cathy stood up so fast that Lucky's ass bounced off the floor. Twice.

"Baron," she repeated, "Is that higher or lower than an Earl?"

There were thirty-seven kids, between the ages of 3 and 18, who lived at Worthinghampton Orphanage. There were plenty of councilors and teachers on hand, but Irene and Aggie made it a habit of supervising every breakfast. It gave them a hands-on feeling for who needed special attention and care. When everyone had been served, they sat down to eat. Chloe sat her tray down across the table from them.

"I need to tell y'all something."

Chloe had been ruder than usual since her stepmother had so cruelly dismissed her. Aggie had suggested that a good pop in the mouth might teach her some manners, but Irene had begged for patience, "There's a sweet, little angel inside there, somewhere," she said.

"I need to establish Fort Worth as my permanent residence," Chloe said, "and I need to transfer from Third Eye Academy to Handley High School."

"Why?" Aggie demanded.

"If you don't mind us asking," Irene added.

"Coach wants me to play for the Handley baseball team next year.

"The girls' softball team?"

"No, Agnes Goodman, I mean the Varsity baseball team. I'm better than any of those guys."

"I don't think," Irene said, reasonably, "with your busy schedule…"

"My schedule will be school and baseball. Period."

"Chloe!" Aggie snapped, "You've got a hundred thousand people passing the hat every Sunday to hear you preach!"

"Fuck that," Chloe responded. "You can take that job and shove it. I quit."

"If you have decided that you must do this," Irene said slowly, "Then you must. I beg you to consider the women who have flocked to the new church to hear you speak, however. You have started a new movement, Chloe. It may not seem so much right now, but remember, that's how the Christian Church began. It was a new message of hope for the poor, the weak, and the forgotten. You've given women from all over this country of ours hope. They are beginning to believe for the first time that they might soon be free of the yoke of Patriarchy. Would you destroy their hopes?"

"Let Alys do it. She believes in Lilith, anyway. She'll preach fiery sermons about revenge. She will encourage those weak-willed women to kill their oppressors."

"No more deaths," Irene objected, "Bonnie turned that lowlife psychopath, Jake, into a martyr. The Wiccan worshippers are wrong. Women are not killers."

"Irene!" Aggie objected. "Don't you see? Women are not one thing or another. We are individuals. We cannot and <u>will not</u> be pigeon-holed any longer. We require a free environment where we can pursue excellence in any field we choose, even baseball."

"SHE HAS A DREAM!" Aggie cried, dramatically.

"OF PLAYING THIRD BASE FOR THE FORT WORTH CATS!" Chloe clarified.

————— ❖ —————

"It seems to me," Lily was saying, "That everything has changed lately. Not just in my life, but everywhere. A year ago, I was in love with Scout and my biggest problem was telling my parents I was gay. Now, I can hardly remember Scout, and my parents…"

For the hundredth time, Lily relived that moment on the stairs with her father. She had known then, and she knew now, that her father had succumbed to his madness. The monster who glared with such intense hatred at her mom was not the man who had carried her home from the hospital when she was born. The last vestiges of humanity had escaped that creature through years of drunkenness and depravity. Lily felt no guilt about his death. She had simply redirected his violent force. He had, karmically, thrown himself off that staircase.

"Every thousand years or so," Martha said, "Humanity experiences a shift in perception. For tens of thousands of years man saw the earth as flat. Then explorers discovered more and more of the world and then, suddenly we all knew that the world was a sphere. It's a phenomenon that happens in different areas. For a hundred years or so, the four-minute-mile was considered impossible. Then someone did it and, suddenly, *everybody* was doing it. It went from 'impossible' to 'commonplace' in a matter of years. It's called a 'Watershed Event' and we are going through one now. Humans are realizing that patriarchy is not a 'natural' state of affairs. In fact, more and more people are waking up to the fact that matriarchy is the only hope for humanity."

The two were motoring through the beautiful forests of East Texas towards Tyler. "We must make sure that Matriarchy is seen in its best light. It behooves us, Martha continued, "to protect feminist leaders such as Alys, who serve feminism with such pride, from any hint of slander.

"Your friend is checking out tomorrow. She didn't seem to enjoy her stay. She barely left her room." Anne sat in the one chair in the little shack I was holed up in. I could sense her boredom.

"Beatrice's life has been almost exclusively an interior one," I replied. It may look boring to us, but she may have spent this weekend on Jupiter being probed by a Polynesian-looking female alien." I could feel Anne's interest slipping away. In another minute she would be gone and would forever be "the one that got away". I stood up and began to disrobe.

"Anne," I asked, "Have you ever heard of 'The Lioness and the Cheese Grater'?

Martha and Lily took the exit right before the Tyler City Limits which led to White-Tail Ranch and my tiny shack.

"She must be able to see us coming," Lily said.

"She may be asleep," Martha answered, "Let's not wake her. Let's just go in."

"When they did, they found Anne riding my face, waving a cowboy hat in her hand and yelling, "Yee-Haw!"

CHAPTER ELEVEN

TALL TALES

Bonnie and Connie liked to sneak out at night and listen to Starr talk of the olden days. Starr was about a hundred years old and had killed dozens of men. Ever since she had been forced into hiding, Starr had lived in the cave next to the renegade monks who worshipped TV.

She always had a gallon jug of Gallo Sangria and when she passed out, Bonnie and Connie would share what was left. Connie was just there for the wine, but Bonnie idolized Starr. She dreamed of, someday, being just like Starr: a hard-hearted, cold-blooded killer.

"Tell us again about the first guy you killed," Bonnie begged.

"I tol' ya, kid. That one wasn't even a real kill. That guy committed 'suicide by cop'. There were a dozen of us FBI agents surrounding him, and the fool pulled a gun on us. I just happened to be the one who shot him. I shot him in the face."

This was the part Bonnie liked, "And it blew up like one of Gallagher's watermelons!" she exclaimed. Connie gave Bonnie a frightened look and Starr took another swig of Sangria straight from the jug.

"McConnel found a piece of bone in his hair," she recited by rote. The horror stories had become trite and boring to her over the years. She thought, at the time, that she would never get over the ugliness of the world of male violence, but she found it didn't bother her anymore.

"How come you quit the FBI?" Bonnie asked.

"I didn't quit. I was fired."

"You? I heard you were their million-dollar baby; young, sexy, and a cold-blooded murderer to boot. Why would they fire you?"

"They said I botched an assignment. I was supposed to kill Cathy Anderson, but they say I shot Aly by mistake, instead."

"I get it. You let your hatred for your former lover override your sense of duty. In the heat of the moment, you couldn't kill Cathy, whom you've always loved, and tried to kill Alys, instead.

"That's some pretty clever psychological conjecture, Dr. Freud, but as I've said for the last twenty years, I didn't shoot Alys. When I got on the scene, Julie Frazier was set up on the second-floor landing to shoot Cathy. I grabbed my weapon and fired a hurried shot at Julie.

It was my only miss in my entire life. Instead of blowing her brains out, the bullet blew her nose off. I would have finished the job, but, right then, someone blew my fake ear off."

"Who?"

"I've heard every crazy theory, from my boss, Captain O'Brien, to the little brunette girl, Sarah. Personally, I'd put my money on Stanley Scovall."

"Whoever it was had set up on top of the old bomb shelter with a tripod and a scope. He (or she) could have taken out anybody in Cathy's house from there. Stanley, of course, had lived next door all his life. He would have known about that spot.

"Starr, I may have had too much Sangria, but the thing with you, Alys, and Cathy has always puzzled me. Were you ever in love with either of them? Both of them?

Starr didn't answer for a long time.

"Did you ever hope that maybe life was a movie, and you were the star?" she finally asked. "I dreamed about that when I was a kid, and when Alys told me she loved me, I thought, 'Wow, it's true! Life is magical! It's a Disney Movie!'

"But Alys was **too good to be true**. She loved intensely, passionately, but indiscriminately. She would never love any one as much as she loved herself.

"Starr, I hate to mention it, but isn't Cathy exactly the same way?"

"The difference is, if I made Cathy a Queen, she'd treat me like a King. If I made Alys a Queen, she would cheat with the footman (or footwoman) just for the fun of it."

Starr didn't speak for a while and the girls started to reach for the jug of Sangria. Then, Starr started and began to ramble on:

"It wasn't my numerous kills that earned me my reputation for cold-heartedness", she said. "What kept me up at night were not the blatant acts of violence she had committed, but subtle lies and innuendoes that might have led to tragedy."

Connie seemed to have a 'sixth sense' that enabled her to sniff out Starr's thoughts. She asked her, "What's the worst thing you ever did?"

"In <u>this</u> lifetime?" Starr joked.

Connie didn't laugh.

Starr took another swig of Sangria and sighed, "I guess it's all water under the bridge now. The harm has been done. Maybe it will be cathartic to talk about it.

She was silent for so long that Connie feared she had already passed out. Then she spoke:

"My heart was broken when I was eighteen." A long silence ensued.

"Well? Go on," Connie insisted.

"I was just waiting to see if Bonnie had some caustic comment to make or wanted to play an imaginary violin."

"I'm not saying nothing," Bonnie replied, "Just don't think I care."

"What I thought that day," Starr continued, "was, 'The world just ended'. With all the drama of Armageddon, Love and Trust collapsed like the Twin Towers on 9/11.

And then, a second went by, my heart beat another beat, and life went on. Twenty years later, I know that **A** world ended that day, but a sadder, drabber world continues.

The world where I believed in true love and happy endings ended that day, but a new world took its place, a world of cynicism and distrust. I became a killer, but before that I was a liar and a backstabber.

When I returned to Denver in 1987, Helen Dunnally very kindly let me stay in Amy's apartment. Amy wasn't there at the time, although Ms. Dunnally said she might return at any time. I had been living there, alone, for a month when she did return. I immediately developed a huge crush on her.

She was like a flat-chested, dark-haired version of Alys. I threw myself at her. I couldn't help it. Whether it was some kind of perverted revenge thing or whether I was just lonely, I don't know. I just know that I pursued Alys's half-sister relentlessly.

The poor child accepted my advances with insouciance. She was bi-sexual and, even before the brain tumor turned her into a raging nymphomaniac, she was always up for recreational sex of any kind.

When I would tire, she would ply me with questions about Alys: Was she really close to her dad, Scott? Did he really buy her a pony?

At first, I would just slightly exaggerate the wonderful things Alys had told me about her dad. He was a great dad. He protected her from her mean mom. He doted on her.

Then, I don't know if it was my hatred of Alys or the emptiness of my life without her that made me do it, but I started making shit up. (The opposite of love might be indifference; but the result of having your heart torn out of your chest is hatred.)

She was a witch. She had put a spell on Scott to prevent him from loving his other children. She had a familiar named Midnight.

The truth was, I didn't expect either of us to ever see Alys, so it didn't matter what I said. Then, in the fall, Amy came into the room with a letter in her hand. She had gone pale. I took the letter and read it."

"This is addressed to me," I said.

Amy sat on my bed and said quietly, "I've been intercepting your mail all summer. Alys has written to you many times, begging you for forgiveness. This came today."

I read:

Dear Starr,

I know you don't read these letters. A few weeks ago, I asked you to "forgive me or tell me to kill myself." I know you, love. I know you couldn't resist doing one or the other. And I think I would have done it if you had told me to. I think so. You don't really know what you will do when the time comes to actually pull the trigger. I don't want to die, but if there is no chance that you will ever forgive me, then I don't want to live either.

There is something that I've kept secret all my life. It's only fair that the one person I really wanted to tell should know. The fact is I'm a murderer, Starr. I killed a boy named Frank when I was fifteen. I shot him six times. If I had stopped after one shot, it would just have been a traumatic experience that I would see a psychiatrist about every week. But... I had a sort of religious experience. Lilith showed me who this worthless bag of shit really was.

He raped me, Starr, and I couldn't forgive him for that. I decided, coolly, calmly, to end him. I passed judgment on him. I executed him. I shot him repeatedly, until I was sure he was dead.

Someone (I can't remember, now, who) suggested that when I kissed Cathy, I knew you would find out; that I was subconsciously punishing myself for being so happy with you when I knew I didn't deserve it. I think it must have been something like that, darling, because I know I would never have done it in my right mind.

Oh, my god. The love we had. It was perfect! I will never love another.

There is no other but you, my love.

I'm not trying to justify my actions, love. I know what I did was unforgivable. I just wanted you to know how screwed up I was back then. In case you don't believe me, I've enclosed a police report from that night. The officer who signed it at the bottom, Jane Hamilton, saved my sanity that night. She held me and promised me that I could someday get over the experience.

She can tell you that this is true. Ask her; then try to forgive me."

With all my love, Alys

Starr laid her head back against a rock and began to snore. The jug of Sangria hung perilously from one finger. Bonnie and Connie rescued it. They passed it back and forth.

"So, her worst thing ever was kissing Cathy," Connie said.

"That was Alys, you idiot. Weren't you listening? Her worst thing ever was lying to Amy about Alys. Alys was never as bad as Amy thought."

They passed the jug back and forth.

"The coolest part was the way Alys killed that dude," Bonnie said, "Can you imagine? She unloaded a clip into him."

"The coolest part," Connie countered, "was when Alys begged Starr for forgiveness though she knew it was too late. That was tragic and romantic."

The girls discussed it until the wine was gone. Then Connie went to her ledge, stripped off her clothes and howled at the moon and Bonnie snuck back into her dorm and slept it off.

What neither of them knew was that Starr hadn't finished her story. The worst thing Starr ever did was tell Amy that the boy Alys killed… was her brother.

Philippa Borgia entered "The Dickinson Dude Ranch" as a tourist. The main drag was, of course, set up like an Old West Main Street. The facades that said **Jail** or **Blacksmith** were expensive boutiques when you walked through the doors. The **Saloon** was (thank God) a real bar. It was cool and dark, and the bourbon on the rocks hit the spot. The Texas Driver's License in her purse said she was "Amelia Crawford", a 30-year-old brunette from Richardson, Texas, and that's exactly who she looked like.

The poseurs who call themselves *Wiccans* and have barely dipped a toe into witchcraft, like to scare themselves with stories of the famous **SHAPESHIFTER**, Philippa Borgia. That made her feel good. She considered herself a master of disguise like Sherlock Holmes. If she was so good that the superstitious gave her credit for magical powers, so much the better.

When the bartender asked her if she wanted another drink, Philippa handed her a $100 bill and told her, "Keep them coming, honey, I'm on vacation."

When she served the next drink, the bartender said, "I'm Wynonna. What are you vacationing from?"

"I'm Amelia, Wynonna. I work at Bell Helicopter. I'm in Account Management. I settle accounts.

Scout was immediately rehired.

"You're the only one she'll listen to," Lucky said. "Cathy has never been good with young

people and I'm just a weird Fortune Teller to her. She's loved you from your first day as nanny."

"It wears off."

"What?"

"The spell. The charm. Whatever it is, it wears off. People fall in love with me the moment they see me, but, sooner or later, they get over me. Just look at Lily."

With that, she burst into tears. Lucky handed her a silk handkerchief with the letters MA embossed on it. Madame Aurora was making a lot of money these days.

"Evidently, my grandmother's rival was a better witch doctor than she was. Granny's protection amulets are worthless. People keep falling in love with me at first sight, then they either go crazy with jealousy like Danny, or forget all about me like Lily."

This brought on a renewed bout of crying and sniffling and nose- blowing that left Lucky with no desire to have her expensive handkerchief back.

"Someone has to talk some sense into Chloe, and you are the only one she'll listen to," Lucky said, fervently.

Scout, granddaughter of a witch doctor, had a bit of a sixth sense, "What's your angle, Lucky?" The question annoyed Lucky, but since she was secretly in love with Scout, she decided to tell her the truth.

"What Chloe calls 'Evangelical Revivals' are really a multi-million-dollar business. The proceeds from that business go into the Chloe Dunnally- Williams Trust Fund, which is the sole source of income for The Lilith Foundation. The Lilith Foundation is run by Cathy Anderson and Cathy gets all her investment advice from Madame Aurora, i.e., *moi.*"

Cathy is just beginning her campaign for Governor and is relying heavily (if not to say, EXCLUSIVELY) on the money that Chloe is raking in for us. She CANNOT quit preaching and go off and play fucking *baseball!* It's crazy. It's idiotic. It's…"

"Costing <u>you</u> money," Scout finished for her. Lucky put her finger on her nose and said, "Bingo!"

"OK, Nancy. I'll do what I can."

Both girls laughed. Lucky had been called by many different names in her lifetime. Her congenital gambler mom had named her 'Lucky', but her customers had called her Lilith and she had answered to many other sobriquets, not the least of which was 'Madame Aurora'. One night, after Cathy had retired, the girls were getting high and listening to old records.

They were listening to an old Beatle song called *Rocky Raccoon* when these lyrics
cracked them up:
"Her name was Magil, and she called herself Lil,
But everyone knew her as Nancy."

Scout's promise came as easily as their shared laugh, but she knew it was almost impossible to change Chloe's mind once it was made up.

No suicide note was ever found at the scene of Starr's mom's suicide. There wasn't one, really. If the authorities had searched Starr's pajamas, they would have found this newspaper clipping:

POLICE SEARCH FOR MISSING BOY

Ten-year-old Frank Stone has reportedly run away from "Mile-High Orphanage", again. Authorities say he told several other orphans that he would never be caught. His parents are unknown, although it is said that a man from back east was questioned about the child when he was born.

THE DENVER POST

Chloe could bat equally well left-handed or right-handed. She threw with her left hand and encouraged her teammates to call her 'Lefty'. She didn't particularly like the nickname; she just hated the name Chloe.

That was the name the hysterical, red-faced girls would scream at the stage when she was performing. "CHLOE-CHLOE-CHLOE" the brainless automatons would chant. (Or **automorons**, as Chloe thought of them.)

Chris Hanlon winked at her as she passed him in the dugout on her way to bat. "Go get 'em, Lefty," he said. Chloe never knew if he was teasing her or not. Sometimes she thought he liked her. Sometimes that thought tied knots in her stomach. Sometimes it made her swing at balls way out of the strike zone. She tried to concentrate.

The first pitch was over her head. She tried to check her swing, but she'd broken her lock on her wrists. "Strike One."

Chloe tapped the bat on the plate and tried to relax.

"You swing like a girl," someone yelled from the stands. Guys seemed to find this hilariously funny. There were masculine laughs and hoots from the stands, the other bench, and even from her own dug-out. Chloe swung as hard as she could at the second pitch. She was in front of the slowball by a mile.

"Strike Two!"

"Dyke!" someone yelled. Did Chloe hear someone say, "just like her mom"? Chloe pounded her bat into home base like it was some bastard's face. It wasn't her mom who was gay! Her mom was named Amy and she was dead. It was her goddamn stepmom who was a lesbian! It was she who got her name all over the gossip pages with all her girlfriends! She smashed the plate so hard the catcher and umpire both stood up and took a step back.

"Sorry," she said and took her place in the batter's box.

She glared into the pitcher's eyes. "Put one over the plate," she dared, telepathically. Maybe he got the message. The next pitch was a 90 MPH fastball right over the plate, waist high. Chloe hit it out of the park.

As her teammates carried her back to the dugout, she saw Chris sitting in the same spot. He winked and said, "Nice hitting, Lefty." Her heart lodged in her throat.

CHAPTER TWELVE

IN FLAGRANTE DELICTO

Anne managed to maintain an air of nonchalance as she dressed. Fortunately, she had little to put on and it didn't take long.

Fully attired in pants, shirt, and sandals, she gave me a peck on the cheek and said, "Thanks for a lovely Tea, dear."

"Come again," I said, with a little giggle.

When Anne had left, Martha introduced Lily, but she wouldn't look at me. Looking at the floor, she said, "Alys, this is Lily Inouye."

Now fully dressed, I walked over to Lily and shook her hand. "I never thought I would say this, but you're even more beautiful than your mother. Did you know she's staying just five miles away? Maybe if you caught a ride with Anne, you could visit with her."

"She checked out early this morning," Martha said, still looking at the floor, "She's on her way back to New York."

"I didn't know she was already gone. Time passes quickly when you're…" I couldn't think of any way to end that sentence and just left it hanging out there.

Lily sat down and very graciously asked, "Did someone mention tea?"

I fussed over the preparation of the tea, while Martha damned me with no praise:

"Mr. Worthinghampton has managed to keep Virgil from shutting the Orphanage down completely, although sponsors are pulling out every day. You can't blame them when the owner has run away in the face of charges that she's corrupting the children with her wicked lifestyle." She glanced at the bed that Anne and I had recently vacated.

"And don't worry about Starr (if you ever did). She's a suspect in a murder case and has been having to hide out in caves. Luckily, some of her friends are there for her. I've hired her the best lawyer I could afford, but she refuses to turn herself in. She says her stepdaughter is in danger and she must save her."

"Chloe's given up preaching," Lily said, conversationally.

"DO WHAT?"

"She's going to play baseball from now on. She says she is going to be the first female professional baseball player."

"Well, that's incredible! Good for her."

"Would you two stop it," Martha said with exasperation, "Chloe is not going to waste her life playing sports. She is in a unique position to influence the fate of Humanity. A million women listen to her and will act as she tells them. She is going to lead the world into the new Age of Matriarchy."

"She's hitting 367," Lily said.

"I've seen her make triple out by herself," I said.

Seeing the dubious look on Lily's face, I began to describe the amazing feat, "She made this incredible leaping catch behind second base, catching the runners in long lead-offs..."

Martha sighed. "I'm dealing with a bunch of kids."

Later, finding nothing but Coors Light and pastrami in the refrigerator, Martha went out for groceries. When we were alone, I apologized to Lily.

"Martha's usually not so grouchy. I don't know what's gotten into her."

"Well, Alys, it's a long drive from Ft. Worth to Tyler. Martha and I did a lot of talking. I may be able to enlighten you on what's eating Martha. It concerns someone named Starr. Starr was hurt badly by a girl named Alys. It seems Alys couldn't keep her vagina in her pants."

"You don't have to tell me anything about the pain I have caused Starr. Who do you think you are? God?"

"As a matter of a fact, there's a voice inside my head telling me I'm Lilith."

The plastic cup I was pouring a 'Coors Light' into flew out of my hand and splashed all over Lily.

"Dumb cunts say, 'What?' I muttered.

"What?" Lily asked, confused (and wet).

"Nothing, nothing. Not your fault. It just slipped out of my hand."

"It didn't slip out of your hand, you degenerate! You threw beer all over me because you are violent and impulsive. Your wicked caprice knows no boundaries. No wonder Starr left you.

"You judge me because you are hung up on your mundane sexual mores and *you can't tell a sexual Revolutionary when you see one!* You are blind to the possibility that *I* was the victim, and Starr was the one trying to imprison me! I loved her, but I found myself staring into the gaping maws of DOMESTICITY!"

This Lily kid was a stranger to me, and I don't think she really knew anything about me. I think it was Lilith's voice I heard next, and not Lily's.

"Oh, here we go. Bring out the loud guitars; she's going to go into her famous 'Free Bird' rant. She's going to lament loudly (and off-key) how her girlfriend couldn't understand that she was chosen by the (female) gods to pleasure every chick in Texas. Who does she think she's fooling? HEY, ALYS! Wake up and smell the smoldering resentment! Nobody has given you carte-blanche to fulfill your carnal lust with every pretty little dixie-chick that comes along. You're not a sexual revolutionary, Alys. You're a selfish cunt!"

"And Lord knows," I said proudly, "I can't change! I gotta be FREE! No Lily, no Lilith, no church, no moral bullies, NOTHING will change the Free Birds of the world."

I snapped my fingers and Lynyrd Skynyrd filled the air around my little cabin in East Texas.

"Lord knows I can't change!"

It was LOUD. It ROCKED. I slung my air-guitar off my shoulders and JAMMED!

Kids out on the streets in Fort Worth and Houston and Glen Rose and Boerne joined in. People in bars and prisons and schools, and back seats of Chevy's all joined in.

Mr. and Mrs. Monogamy,

If you don't happen to like it, FUCK YOU!

———◦❊◦———

Dawn and Misty were exhausted when they entered the office of Sappho Security Services. They found Bonnie in the waiting room watching Jerry Springer. They heard loud snoring coming from under the reception desk.

"We're closed," Bonnie said, without taking her eyes off the TV. Then, glancing at Misty, she said, "We ain't accepting runaways at this time." Then Bonnie's eyes lit up and she smiled like she'd thought of something funny, "On account of all the adults have run away." There was a barking noise from under the reception desk.

"I'm no runaway," Misty responded, "I'm a deputy. This here is US Marshall Jan Sprat and, if that's marijuana I smell, I'm putting you under arrest."

A naked 15-year-old girl scrambled out from under the reception desk and sped out the back door. She had the hairiest bush Dawn had ever seen. Dawn sat in the chair next to Bonnie. She stretched her legs out and crossed them at the ankles. "What's your name, kid?" she asked.

"Bonnie."

"Bonnie, why was 6 afraid of 7?"

"Because 7 ate 9, and that joke was old when I first heard it when I was 6."

"Well, we've come from a land far, far away. We're very tired. We seek a girl named Lily. You haven't seen her, have you?"

"Pretty Polynesian chick, mid-twenties?"

"Yes! That's her!"

"No. Haven't seen her."

"Bonnie!"

"OK. OK. She and Martha went to a Dude Ranch just south of Tyler. Some evil witch has threatened Chloe. They are going down there to protect her."

The chair that Dawn sat in was pretty comfortable as far as waiting room chairs went. She slumped back into it and rested her head on the back. "How far is it to Tyler?" she asked."

It's about a two-hour drive."

"Well, shit. I'm just going to rest my eyes for a minute."

When she opened them, two hours later, Nan Butler found herself looking at her old fuckbuddy, Starr Williams.

"Hey Slim, how's tricks?"

"Nan?" Dawn didn't look anything like Nan, but that phrase was exactly what Nan would have said to Starr.

In that much time, Dawn had become fully awake. "I'm sorry, ma'am. I thought for a minute…"

"That's OK, kid." Starr seemed to let it go. Then, she said suddenly, "What rhymes with orange."

"No, it doesn't."

Alys had been bugging Starr, and everyone else, about Dawn being the reincarnation of Nan. Now Starr was beginning to wonder.

"Come with me to my humble castle in the skies," she said to the young girl, "while I pack a few belongings.

The two walked out the back of the Worthinghampton Inn and up a steep path that led to the Worthinghampton Orphanage. They didn't speak until they had passed through the almost deserted orphanage and begun walking up another steep path.

"I didn't kill Hecate Collins, Na…um, Dawn."

"I didn't for a second think you did, Starr."

"Because you know I'm not the kind of person who would do that, right?"

"Because I know you're a professional and you wouldn't have left clues all over the place."

They walked the rest of the way to Starr's cave without talking.

"This is what they mean when they say, 'The silence was deafening,'" Dawn said.

"Listen, Dawn…"

Dawn reached out and took Starr's hand. "I have no regrets," she said, "I sense that there was something between us in a previous life. And I think we were both in love with Alys. I suspect we may have hurt her in some way."

"She deserved everything she got."

"I know, but…"

"Besides," Starr added with a big grin on her face, "she loved every minute of it!"

"She did, didn't she?" Nan laughed.

The two young ladies were in a good mood as they packed Starr's few belongings and left the cave.

As they passed the monk's cave, a NEWS ALERT blared from the omniscient TV: A MADMAN HAS ESCAPED FROM THE LADY BUG HOME FOR THE CRIMINALLY INSANE JUST OUTSIDE OF COLLEGE STATION, TX.

Reporting for KIKK news, Shirley Knott says a huge black man has escaped and is holding a hostage.

"Shirley, have there been any developments in the last thirty seconds?"

"Yes, Les. We have an update. Earlier reports of a black man being involved have turned out to be the usual knee-jerk bullshit. Authorities now say that the escaped lunatic, Julie Frazier has disguised herself as a plebe and blended into the crowd on the Texas A&M campus.

Head of Security at the Insane Asylum, Mishubishi "Lil" Kim, has just released this statement:

"Hell, they all look the same to me. We know she's the twelfth man; we just don't know which one."

"Back to you, Les."

Visitors to the Dickerson Dude Ranch are mostly day-trippers. However, those with plenty of money to spend can stay a week or even more without leaving the park. For those not into camping in East Texas Piney Woods, there is a motel on the south side of the Ranch. The facade of the Alamo Hotel entrance is a replica of the famous fort. The walls of the ersatz fort are rooms to rent.

Cathy had checked into Room 147. She and her spiritual advisor, Madame Aurora would stay there. Chloe and Scout would stay in Room 145 if they even came. Both were angry with her. Both had told her what she could do to herself when they got the invitations.

"Don't be silly," she had replied, "I have staff to do that." She smiled at Lucky, who was listening in. Lucky threw a pillow at her.

In that phone conversation, Cathy had pleaded with Chloe to come.

"I promise you I will not try to get you to change your mind. I know your choice of baseball as a career is final and irrevocable. I respect that. But you are the closest thing I've ever had to a daughter, and, frankly, the only person under 30 I've ever liked. Please come spend two weeks with me just having fun."

Chloe knew that Cathy just wanted some publicity photo ops with her while she was still famous as an evangelist, but Chloe had a secret reason for wanting to go. Chris Henson and his family were going to be there!

Cathy didn't know that Scout's love for Lily had turned to hate. When she let it drop that Lily would be there, Scout feigned delight:

"I can't wait to see her. I have a lot to tell her."

Starr, Dawn, and Misty were the last to arrive. After they had settled themselves into Room 146, Starr mixed herself a stiff drink, picked up the phone, and dialed Room 145. When Chloe answered, Starr asked her, "Did you know the Alamo had a pool?"

"Starr?"

"Yeah, apparently, when Travis drew the line in the sand, they were choosing up sides for a game of Water Polo. It's right in the middle of the courtyard. Meet me out there in about ten minutes...I mean, if you want to."

Cathy looked at her old friend in amazement. "You're not going to be a good mom, are you?"

"Stepmom. And fuck you. It's a far, far better thing I do…"

Ten minutes later, Starr and Chloe were sitting out by the pool.

"Stop fidgeting."

"Sorry, Starr, we've never had a heart-to-heart conversation, before. In fact, I can't remember us *ever* having a conversation."

"Chloe, in two weeks, you'll be thirteen."

(Actually, she would be fourteen, but Chloe was amazed that Starr had remembered her birthday at all.)

"Your mother and I were very close, once."

"Like sisters?"

"I wouldn't say that, exactly, but we were very close. Your mom made me promise that I would give you a message. So, here it is. She told me to tell you that you are the 333rd incarnation of Lilith, First Woman, Equal of Adam, and, well, there is more, but that's the gist. Basically, you are Lilith. Nice talk."

Starr got up and returned to her room. Chloe sat there a while, processing. She was in a bit of a daze when she returned and accidentally entered Room 144.

She burst into the room and froze. At first all she could see was the naked figure of Wynonna Boone kneeling by the bed as if in prayer. For a full ten seconds her eyes refused to process the impossible image they saw.

Wynonna was performing cunnilingus on a monster! Its legs were green and scaly, as was the rest of the beast. Its teats hung like saddlebags over a visible ribcage. The green hands that held Wynonna's head and urged her on were slimy and each ended in three sharp claws.

The long dark hair of the hag was in disarray, the mouth red with sharpened white teeth. Her nose was large and bent and had a huge mole on it.

The ecstasy of sex had removed the layers of disguise from the shape shifter and left 'Amelia's' true visage. Her glowing black eyes met Chloe's. She raised her hand. Suddenly, Lily Hardy burst into the room and grabbed Chloe. She thrust the girl behind her and spoke to the witch:

"YOU WILL NOT HARM THIS CHILD!"

And then, as if waking from a dream, Chloe peeked around Lily and saw a tourist from Fort Worth having sex with a bartender from a local bar. The obviously drunk bartender raised her head from what she was doing and said, "Do you mind?"

But, when Lily had backed them up to the door and turned to leave, Chloe looked at the older woman and heard, in her head, the woman say,

"Later, my pretty."

CHAPTER THIRTEEN

ily didn't let go of Chloe until they were in Room 146. Lily pushed Chloe towards Misty and said, "Don't take your eyes off her. I have to go warn Cathy and Lucky that Philippa is here.

"Don't forget Scout," Chloe said, "She's in Room 145."

"Scout's here?" Lily asked. "Oh, shit."

"You go get Cathy and her fortune teller." Misty suggested, "I'll get Scout."

Before Misty had even begun to speak, Starr had run out of the room. They didn't need to ask where she was going.

When Starr burst into Room 144, she found Wynonna Boone sitting on the bed, pulling on her snakeskin cowboy boots.

"Where's Philippa?" Starr asked her.

"You mean Amelia? She got an emergency call from work, or so she said. If you ask me, this fake Alamo doesn't have enough privacy. Maybe that's why the Mexicans overran the place; nobody ever locked the doors! Anyway, she left. I doubt she'll be back." The woman sighed and said, "Too bad!" Starr searched the place but found nothing other than some green slime running down the bedpost.

Starr walked back to 146 just as Misty was introducing Lily to Dawn. Dawn suddenly knelt in front of Lily and said. "Messiah, please accept me as your humble disciple."

Lily took a step back and said, "Lady would you please stand up and quit embarrassing everyone?"

Dawn looked up, surprised. Then she stood up and said sheepishly, "I'm sorry. It's just that the first time you appeared before me you held a fire in your hand and had a dragon on your shoulder. Your natural beauty was magnified. You foretold that I would be your Protector one day."

"You must be thinking about Lilith. I'm just Lily and you can 'protect' me anytime," she said with a wink.

"You admire her?" Scout put a hand on Dawn's shoulder, and glowering at Lily, continued: "Well, I feel sorry for you. Your idol has feet of clay. She's the two-faced god Janus who will 'Build you up just to let you down.'[4]

"You're looking good, Scout."

"Don't talk to me, you dirty slut-whore! I happen to know that you fucked the witch that's trying to kill Chloe! How does that work, exactly? Do you do it on broomsticks…or WITH broomsticks?'

"Hi, I'm Misty."

Chloe turned around to the skinny little street urchin who had tapped her on the shoulder, "Hi, I'm Chloe."

"Hey, Chloe, as much fun as it is to watch the adults make fools of themselves, do you want to explore this tourist trap?"

"Sounds like fun."

Chloe and Misty exited the Alamo Hotel and were immediately shot by half- a-dozen 9 and 10-year-olds who had just purchased their cap guns at The General Store. Their moms had paid $9.99 for the same cap guns they could have bought at K-Mart for $2.99. These, however, said "I made my last stand at DICKERSON'S DUDE RANCH" on the side.

Ma's Home Cooking turned out to be a McDonald's once you got inside, and the girl's stopped there and got a Coke.

---

[4] "The Cheater" Bob Kuban

"There's an arcade just outside of this Hicksville," Misty told Chloe.

"Great! Let's take some water bombs up on the Ferris Wheel."

"Sounds like fun. Only one problem, you got any money?"

"Pfft. That ain't no problem. Give me a street corner and a Bible; and, in two hours, I'll **BUY** that fucking arcade!"

Virgil led Stanley Scovall from the dark alley into the basement of the Sagamore Hill Baptist Church. A dozen men applauded as he entered.

"Gentlemen, once again our Way of Life is being threatened. Our enemy this time is an insidious one that has been around since the beginning. When we threw off the cruel bonds of the British Monarchy- they were there, waiting. When we whipped the Krauts-twice! - They were there at our sides biding their time.

The Arabs got in a lucky sucker punch at 9-11, but since then we've kicked their asses in two Gulf Wars and a bunch of "-stans".

But now our biggest enemy has stepped out into the open. WOMEN, my friends, have declared open war on MEN! Their new Messiah is Lilith, who claims to have been Adam's equal in the Garden of Eden. She has taken the form of a woman called 'Alys'. She and her perverted succubus, Anne Baldwin, threaten to take our children from us and brainwash them in their atheistic, socialistic, lesbianistic ways! They have to stopped, my friends. It's our duty as True Americans to put an end to Alys and Anne."

Misty and Chloe sat on the fence that made up the corral outside the blacksmith's shop. Fake cowboys were scheduled to have a fake gunfight in fifteen minutes and the girls wanted to be sure they had good seats. "You got a boyfriend?" Misty asked Chloe.

"I don't know. Maybe. There is one boy that makes me feel kinda funny and reach for outside balls, but I don't know if he likes me."

"Wow. Well, I gotta tell you, Chloe, before you go reaching for outside balls, I think you should ask him."

"What? Just come right out and, like: "Hey, Chris. Do you like me? I don't think so.""

Just then Misty froze. "Oh, fuck. That's her," she whispered.

Chloe looked across the street to where Misty was looking. She didn't have to ask Misty who she was talking about. The tall, elegant woman with the alabaster skin and the long black hair entering the Cowboy Casino was obviously a woman of great power. She was not your average tourist.

Chloe stood up. "Let's go say 'Howdy'," she said.

"ARE YOU FUCKING KIDDING ME?" Misty's reply was loud enough to turn every head in the place. Mothers covered their kid's ears with a reproving look at Misty. "That is Philippa Borgia," she continued, barely above a whisper, "She's come here to kill you!"

"I doubt she'll try anything in public. Besides, if she does…" Chloe smiled as she revealed the pearl-handled switchblade she had taken out of her pocket. She pressed a button and a 5-inch blade popped out. It looked very sharp.

"Let's give her a warm Texas welcome," Chloe laughed. This was not the monster Chloe had thought she saw in Room 144. This was an assassin with a political agenda. Chloe was no more afraid of her than she was of an eighty-mph fastball.

Philippa was just going to get a thousand dollars' worth of chips. She had decided that if she didn't find anybody fun by the time that was gone, she would just drive back to Tyler for the night and come back tomorrow. Just as she was getting the cash out of her purse, she saw someone she recognized.

Little Misty Whatshername from Seattle and some cute kid she'd never seen before were trying to get into the casino. The bouncer was laughing at their ID's.

Philippa told the lady behind the booth she had changed her mind and went to exit. She walked out as the two dejected girls walked away.

"Hey, Misty," she cried out, "Whatcha doing in Texas?"

The girl turned around and her eyes bulged. She took a couple of backwards steps before she could speak. "Hi, uh…"

"Amelia," Philippa finished for her, "Here in Texas my name is Amelia. Any problem with that?"

"None whatsoever, Amelia."

The other girl was staring intently at 'Amelia'. There was no fear on her face. Her right hand stayed in her pocket. Philippa had no doubt there was a weapon of some kind in that pocket.

"Who's your pretty young friend?" Philippa asked. "She's…"

"Straight." Chloe finished for her.

"And an impertinent child," Philippa said.

"We better be going," Misty said.

As the two teenage girls walked away, Philippa froze Chloe with her parting words:

"Later, my pretty."

"Hello, Lily, my name is Anne Baldwin. I don't know if you remember me. We met briefly."

"Of course, I remember you, Anne. You were the lady who was riding Alys's face the first time I saw you. How could I ever forget you?"

"Yeah. Well, I'm actually calling you on behalf of Alys. I don't know how aware you are of her circumstances, but suffice it to say, she is all alone in that cabin. She needs someone to talk to. She calls me four or five times a day, but the fact is, it's deer season and I'm terribly busy at the Nineteenth Hole. The last time she called, she wanted to do phone sex and, frankly, I'm just not into that. I'm getting worried about her. I don't think masturbating four or five times a day will do her any physical damage, but I worry about her mental health. I was just wondering if you could spend some time with her?"

"And do what exactly?"

"What do you mean?"

"WHAT DO I MEAN? You call me and say your fuckbuddy is lonely and sexual frustrated and then, ask me to spend time with her. I gotta tell you, it seems like you're trying to pimp me out."

"Oh, no. No, no. I'm sorry. I'm telling this all wrong and I've got it all screwed up again. No, no, let me back up a little. My employer, Mr. Worthinghampton has recently informed me that a group called "Make America STRAIGHT Again" has begun a nationwide search for Alys. They say she is a witch and are threatening to burn her at the stake when they find her. I'm very concerned about her safety.

I remembered that when I saw you, I was impressed by your obvious strength. I've never seen a girl with such prominent biceps. I asked around and discovered that you were not only strong, but tough. I thought you could provide company for Alys as well as protection."

"When you were asking around, did you happen to hear I was a lesbian?"

"OK. That came up. But it's not the main thing, Lily. I mean, if you two hit it off, that would be great, but I'm not playing matchmaker here. I'm just asking that you be companionable. What do you say?"

"I'd like to help, Anne, but there is a killer running loose here at the Dude Ranch. She's gunning for Chloe, and I can identify her. I think I'm needed here to protect Chloe.

"Chloe? Chloe quit. It's Alys that the men are after."

"So, who are the witches after?"

"Um, YOU!

Mannie and Mo stepped off the bus three miles south of Tyler on SH69. Manny looked at the words on the bottom of the sheet of paper that had guided him to this point. DESTROY AFTER READING, it said.

"Here, Mo, eat this."

"Homer," Mo replied and ate the paper.

The instructions were from District Attorney Virgil Wilder.

They had been written several days before. The first thing on the list was to report to Stanley, himself, for further instructions. Manny wasn't sure how to do that. Mo had no suggestions. Manny saw an old gentleman who looked like someone reliable and approached him.

"Excuse me, sir. Do you know where Stanley Scovall might be?"

"Well, hello there, young man. I'm Hugo Fughov from Wyoming. My wife Estelle and I are on vacation. You haven't seen her, have you? Last I saw her was in Little Rock. If you see her, tell her I'm heading for Albuquerque. See you later."

Mo pointed across the street to a sign that said: <u>The Line in the Sand</u>. Mo could spot a bar a mile away.

When Wynonna Boone asked him what he wanted, he said, "Give me two whiskeys, please…and a beer for my friend, Mo, here."

About four or six whiskeys later, Manny got down to business.

"I'm looking for a fella name of Scovall, Stanley Scovall. He might be in the guise of a Baptist preacher. Said he was…"

"Ain't seen him."

Mo laid two twenties on the bar.

"There was a preacher man in here a couple a nights ago. Went by the name of Brother Leroy. He was looking for a couple of women."

"Man after my own heart," Manny declared.

"I remember him because he ended up leaving with an ugly redhead dressed in an Aggie cadet uniform. Girl was ugly! I told her so, too.

"You ugly," I said.

"You're drunk," she said back, all high and mighty.

"Yes ma'am, I am, but I'll be sober in the morning, and you'll still be ugly."

Lily found Starr out by the pool.

"Anne's worried about Alys.. She says that assassins are gathering to attack her cabin."

"Why are they attacking Alys?"

"Because she's Lilith."

"Nu-uh. My stepdaughter is Lilith. Her mom, Amy, told me so."

"Well, that drug-addled student, Dawn, thinks I am Lilith."

"My old fuck-buddy, Lucky tells Cathy that SHE is Lilith."

"SHE Lucky or SHE Cathy?"

"Fuck. I don't know."

"What do you think we ought to do?"

"Have you ever seen Alys get drunk and play air-guitar to *Free Bird?* It's a hoot. Let's go there and protect her and get her drunk."

"Sounds like a plan."

They got in Starr's Land-Rover and took off.

The office of the Alamo Motel is next to the pool. There is a room abutting it that is used mostly for birthday parties and such. Occasionally, the rare business conference is held there. It seats twelve comfortably.

Lucky (or 'Madame Aurora'), Cathy, Scout, Misty, Kitty, and Chloe were using the room for a 'War Conference'.

"That witch that killed Hecate is here," Lucky began, "She is going after Chloe, now. Anybody have any idea what we should do?"

"Where is Lily?" Scout asked.

Nobody answered.

"Doesn't it seem sort of suspicious," Scout continued, "that Philippa shows up and Lily disappears?"

Everyone agreed that was highly suspicious although nobody could think what was suspicious about it.

"Well, for Heaven's sake," Scout expostulated, "It's obvious that the lovers are in cahoots. Lily is trying to protect the witch's identity."

"That's a good point," Chloe said, "Although I've seen her, and Misty's seen her..."

"She's a shape-shifter," Misty said.

"I highly doubt that," Lucky said, "and, if she can shape-shift, then having Lily around wouldn't make any difference. She could be you," she said, looking at Scout.

"Or you!" Chloe screamed, tickling Misty.

"Or you!" Misty laughed.

They wrestled around on the floor, trying to rip each other's clothes off, and laughing, "Show your true self, witch."

"JUST TELL THE OLD CRONE SHE'S WON."

It was the authority of Cathy's voice, as much as the volume that got everyone's attention.

"She wants Chloe gone, so we'll go. Madrid is nice this time of year. I'll take her there. Chloe has no interest in politics, witches, or the church. She has no dog in this fight. After a year in Europe, she will return in time to endorse me for Governor and, who knows, by then she might even be attractive."

Cathy's plan was unanimously adopted (unless Chloe's "I've got your *attractive* right here" counts as a 'nay') and the meeting was adjourned.

After the meeting, Lucky asked Dawn if she had a weapon.

"I had to return my ROTC rifle, but I still have my 'side piece'."

"Make sure you keep it on you and loaded until we can get Chloe out of here."

"Of course, we'll need to be armed when we arrest Philippa for questioning in the Hecate Collins murder," Dawn said.

"Right, we'll do that. Then, we'll kill her."

CHAPTER FOURTEEN

OMENS AND PORTENTS

Stanley rolled over in the bed and opened his eyes. The first thing he saw was his noseless girlfriend, Julie Frazier. A shudder of revulsion ran through him. He had remained loyal to Julie for two reasons. One was that he felt partially responsible for her deformity: he had hesitated for just a second before he shot Starr. He had hesitated because he knew if he stopped Starr, his dearest friend in the world, Cathy, would surely die.

Then, after that brief instant, his duty to country and God forced him to go through with it. He pulled the trigger. If he hadn't hesitated his dear Julie would still have a nose; but Cathy would be dead. (The second reason he remained loyal to Julie was that both before her rhinoplastic disaster, and after, she gave the best head he had ever had.)

Perhaps in another, parallel universe, Julie slept on, and the couple lived happily ever after; but, in this particular universe, Julie woke up. And she woke up grouchy.

"You were hitting on that bartender last night."

"Bartender?" Men, take note. This is an excellent tactic for when your partner is attacking you. Remain vague and distracted, as if you don't really know what she's talking about. Don't add to the conversation; just keep repeating what she says in a confused and innocent manner. In the end, her own fury and frustration will cause her to something dumb like throw a brush at you. Hopefully, it will hit you in the head.

Then, you can go around rubbing your head and looking hurt until <u>she</u> feels remorse.

"Yes. You know the one I'm talking about. The horsey one with the big rack. The one who called me ugly!"

"Remember guys, nothing beats 'Stout Denial': "Who are you going to believe; me, or your lying eyes?""

"Oh, um." Stanley did remember that bartender. She came across as a 'good ol' country girl' but there was something about her, something exciting. She seemed to glow with a secret sexuality that stirred his phenomes. Dirty, nasty sex seemed to ooze out of her pores.

He thought of her as he looked at Julie. Nobody looks their best first thing in the morning, but when their prosthetic nose is askance; it's the absolute worst. Stanley made up his mind. *Tomorrow,* he vowed, *I'll wake up next to Wynonna Boone.*

"It's over, Julie."

When Starr and Lily walked into my little cabin, I very nearly had a heart attack. "The Love of My Life" stood like a dim, insignificant shadow next to the glowing Polynesian Goddess that appeared before me. (Sadly, alas <u>tragically</u>, those are ironic air-quotes that surround the name of my once beloved Starr.) For now, I knew no love but Lily.

Lily Hardy was every bit as beautiful as her mother, Beatrice Inouye, had been twenty years earlier. As Moses descended Mt. Sinai with the new laws, so I descended into mundane reality knowing that everything had changed. I realized that Starr had spoken:

"Martha is convinced that the men intend to kill you. She has asked us to protect you."

"You are Lily," I said, ignoring Starr.

"And you are Alys, the founder of the Church of Lilith," she replied.

Starr noisily checked the magazine of her Walther PPK, and stalked out saying, "I'm going to check the perimeter."

Lily and I stood facing each other and the future. I didn't want to make small talk about her time as a cheerleader. I didn't want to know about her childhood. And I particularly did not want to mention I knew her mom (biblically). I decided to cut to the chase.

"Lily, did you kill your dad?" I thought I knew the answer to this question, but Lily's answer knocked the wind out of my sails.

"No, I didn't kill him; Lilith did."

The first thing Philippa did when she got to the Dickinson Dude Ranch was troll the streets for working girls. She used the local hookers as a sort of 'Baker Street Irregulars'. She met Nadia within an hour of her arrival. She was surprised that the girl seemed more interested in whether the air-conditioning in her motel room was working than the price she would be paid.

"When the A/C is broke," she said, "the work is even more unbearable."

"Well, gee, thanks. I thought you girls enjoyed the work. I thought that was why you did it."

"On the contrary, I came to the Dude Ranch to escape debauchery. I wanted legitimate work. I'll tell you, I've heard "You Can't Go Home Again", but I think it's because you can never leave home in the first place."

Philippa cut the girl off before she could wax poetic. "You won't have to do any of that kind of work for the next few days. All you need to do is keep your eyes and ears open for information leading to the termination of one Alys Loxley."

"I may have to charge double." She had obviously heard of the Legendary Lesbian Lothario.

"Just listen. All you have to do is find out where Alys or her friend Chloe are staying. If you get this information, you will make more in the next few days than you do with a convention of Shriners in town."

Lilith spoke to me for the first time since Nan's funeral.

"Lily had a lifetime of Christian indoctrination to deal with. When 'push' came to 'shove', well, she needed a little help."

"So, you shoved him off the stairs?"

"Alys, you know I'm a disembodied spirit. I cannot cause a physical action in the material world."

"So, how did you kill him, Lilith?"

"I merely showed him in his own mind's eye, what he looked like to his daughter. He took a header off the stairs after that."

I looked at the beautiful Lily and gave her my hard-earned knowledge. "If you take a life, karma will take the life of someone you love."

"I tell you, Alys. I did not kill him."

"Well, that's good, Lily. I'm hoping you and I will be friends. I'm hoping we will be *extremely close* friends, but first, I have to clear up one thing about your new friend, Lilith. She's not as powerful as she might want you to think. When she and I started the church, we had a handful of people. It wasn't until an entrepreneurial little brat named Chloe thought it would be fun to convert to Lilithianism that the church had any following to speak of. Whatever Lilith wants, she's going to make you do all the hard work."

"I'm not afraid of hard work, Alys. I've worked the base of the pyramid in one-hundred-degree Texas heat."

"You know, I once worked the base of an Eiffel Tower with a police officer and an FBI assassin, but I'm not bragging about it."

"I wasn't bragging."

"Come on. It's second nature for TCU girls to brag. Y'all think you are better than us poor girls."

"I don't think I'm better..."

"Prove it by having dinner with me at Denny's tonight."

"Well, I don't know."

"Snob."

"Oh OK, fine."

Starr came in from making her rounds. "You always did like them young," she commented.

"Did you see any men lurking out in the bushes?" I asked.

"No, but speaking of bushes, there are a couple of girls approaching and one of them is naked. She's got the hairiest bush I've ever seen."

"Sounds like Connie. She'll be good for sniffing out predators.

Actually, the first thing Connie sniffed out were some left-over T-bones in my trash can. She curled up in the corner of the kitchen and gnawed on them, contentedly. Bonnie ran up to Starr and said, "Hey Agent Williams, I killed my first man last Saturday."

"That's nice, kid, but you're supposed to have legal authorization before you do that."

"The guy attempted to rape Connie."

"Oh, well. As long as there was a good reason…"

"Why are you here?" I asked Bonnie.

"The lady at the 19th Hole said you needed female companionship."

"Anne is really good to me, but here's the thing, Bonnie. I've got Starr, Lily, Dawn, and, sometimes, Anne, here to protect me. My little shack is getting crowded. Why don't you put some clothes on Connie and head down to the "Dickinson Dude Ranch"? I need you and Connie to keep your eyes peeled for witches. Can you do that?"

"Anything for you, Alys. If you had forced me to go back home to my stepfather, one of us would be dead by now. The best day of my life was the day you sent me down to the Orphanage and I met Connie. I'll kill every witch in the Dude Ranch if you want me to."

"Naw, don't kill 'em; just keep an eye on them, OK?"

"Kay."

CHAPTER FIFTEEN

SCHRODINGER'S QUEEN

Misty was not so much in love with Chloe, as in awe of her. Not that she knew anything about Chloe's fame as a child-evangelist, she had just never seen a kid talk back to adults the way Chloe did. She acted as if she were their equal. She was totally fearless.

Misty thought Chloe's plan to hunt down Philippa and confront her was ill-conceived and ill-advised. "You've seen her true visage. You know that she is a monster," she told her, "Why would you be willing to face her without Lily around?"

"Do you think Lily is pretty?"

"She is, without a doubt, the most beautiful woman I've ever seen, and that includes movies and magazines. But what has that got to do with anything? Why do you ask?"

"What if she is a shape-shifter? What if her true visage is worse than Philippa's? What if we are ALL shape shifters? Maybe we all present false facades to others. Maybe if she weren't so damn pretty, everybody wouldn't love her so much! The image I saw of Philippa was my own imagination. I heard a witch was coming here from the Pacific Northwest, and I conjured a monster in my own mind.

Everybody knows that area has witches, survivalists, and Sarah Palin, oh my! There's no such thing as shift-shapers"

"Shape shifters."

"Whatever. If Philippa could change shape at will, she could anybody. She could be him!"

With that, she shoved an eight-year-old boy onto the ground.

When the kid burst into tears, she said, "No, just a kid. If he were her, he would have shot me with this." She took the kid's cap pistol away from him and shot him 4 or 5 times. Misty pried the toy out of Chloe's hand and gave it back to the crying child.

Then she led Chloe away from the irate parents.

"You can't do shit like that," she hissed.

"Oh, you'd be surprised at the things I can do," she said, as she led Misty into the Dickinson Diner. "Depending on how fast you can run, I might even be able to get us some free breakfast."

As they were being led to a table, Chloe suddenly froze. Misty felt sure she must have seen the witch. A guy rose from one of the tables they were passing.

"Hello, Chloe," Chris Hanlon said, "These are my parents. Mom, Dad, meet my friend, Chloe."

Misty slathered the soft, fluffy waffles with syrup. Her bacon was crisp, just the way she liked it. It may very well have been the best meal she had ever eaten. Between huge mouthfuls, she addressed the pale, almost comatose, figure across the table from her:

"You know, I grew up on the hard streets of Seattle, fighting for survival, but I swear to God, I'm more socially graceful than you. You <u>do not</u> curtsy in a diner! Speak, goddamn it! You haven't said one coherent word since we ran into your boyfriend.

Chloe managed to focus her eyes and ask Misty, "What did he say?"

"I've told you five times, already."

"He said, 'My friend, Chloe', didn't he? Didn't he?

"Yes, and then you said 'um' and 'ah' and a lot more incomprehensible gibberish until I had to lead you away like a blathering idiot."

A cloud covered Chloe's usually imperturbable face. "I didn't look stupid, did I?"

Misty let it go.

"He said he'd meet us at the amusement park at ten," Misty reminded Chloe.

"OMG! What will I wear? Do you have any make-up?"

"Are you going to eat those eggs?"

Two hours later they stood inside the entrance to the amusement park waiting for Chris. Chloe was beginning to get worried. Misty had been worried since they left the Alamo.

"I wish you would let me call Dawn and tell her where we are," Misty said, "I'm sure everyone is worried about us. If Dawn were here, she would protect us. She was studying to be a cop; you know. She's pretty tough."

"I think she has a crush on Lily."

"I think so too, and I think Lily likes her back."

"How much do you really know about Dawn?" Chloe asked her.

"Well, I know she tells the worst jokes in the world, but not much more than that."

"I don't want to disillusion you, or anything, but your friend Dawn is just one on a long list of Alys's conquests."

"Alys and your Mom? OMG!"

"Yeah, and the story is that they all got together with for a threesome!"

[Alys Note]- *This story (like 90% of the shit Chloe says) is patently false. Dawn is, like, half our age. Now, Nan. Well, that's a different story.*

"No Way! Do you mean Alys Loxley, the Legendary Lesbian Lothario? She's quite famous in the Northwest. They call her the 'Black Widow Spider' in Seattle because, if a man has sex with her, she kills him."

"It's true! I saw the mini-series on LifeTime Channel!"

"But your mom's not like Alys. I mean, she must like men because, well, she had you."

"No, dumbass. Starr's not my mom, she's just my <u>step</u>mom. She just adopted me after my real mom died."

"And your real mom was?"

"Amy Dunnally. Whose father was Scott Loxley."

"Loxley? Like in Alys Loxley?"

"He was Alys's father and my mother's biological father."

"So, he's your biological grandfather."

"Yeah, and get this: My stepmother's mother was a grafter who worked with him and Amy's mom.

"Holy Shit! This whole thing is as incestuous as Fuck!"

"And the Queen of all Lesbos is Senator Cathy Anderson who wants me to endorse her as the next Governor of Texas."

"She's gay?"

"Not to hear her talk. She claims to be straight. What a hypocrite!"

"Perhaps it all depends on how you look at it," Chris Hanlon said, walking up behind the girls. "Like Schrodinger's cat. "You," he said, looking at Chloe, "look at Cathy and see a dead cat. You," he said, waving toward Misty, "see a live cat. Perhaps, before either of you open her box, she exists in a state of quantum superposition where she is neither dead nor alive.

"Or," he concluded with a big grin, "she's just a lady who wishes to be Queen."

[Hello, it's me, your omniscient narrator, with an observation: Women always have and always will, compete for the attention of a male. It doesn't matter if the girls are gay or straight, young, or old; they crave male attention. The competition is not always fair, though.]

"Hello, Chris," Chloe said coquettishly.

"So, the cat refuses to be defined by preconceived notions," Misty blustered desperately.

"Exactly." Chris agreed.

"People should be judged on the contribution they make to society, rather than any arbitrary attribute such as physical beauty or sexual proclivity," Misty concluded brilliantly.

Chloe chose to take the low ground. "She's gay and I'm straight."

She and Chris spent the rest of the evening getting to know one another better.

Misty wandered off and got kidnapped.

The <u>Book of Lilith</u> (which claims to be the Divinely Inspired Word of God) says that Nadia called Philippa and said, "Philippa, it's me, Nadia. The girls you had me shadowing are splitting up. The one called

Chloe hid out in the Tunnel of Love with the guy. The other one, Misty, is hanging outside the liquor store trying to get someone to buy her some booze. Which one do you want me to stay with?"

"You get Misty. Get her drunk and take her to your place. I may need a human sacrifice later, and you know how hard it is to find virgins these days. I'll take over surveillance of Chloe and the male. I have a feeling they will be there for a while.

Misty woke in a dirty bed in a filthy room. She had never been roofied before. She was relieved to find, upon examination, that not only was she still intact, so were the contents of her purse. There was nobody else in the room but a cat. The cat was curled up at the end of the bed by her feet.

"Hey, little puss, what's going on?"

Misty got up and went to the door. It was locked. There was a window, but it was up around the ten-foot ceiling which made Misty think she might be in some kind of underground bunker. A faint light filtered through the dirty glass of the window.

"Looks like we're locked in here, puss."

The cat rolled on its back and stretched. Then it rolled back over into a ball and went back to sleep.

"Yeah, you're right. We may as well make the best of it." Misty sat on a rickety chair by a scarred-up table. "We'll just have to wait until your master, or whoever feeds you, comes home.

Then Misty paused.

Ever since she had heard the word "epiphany", she had wanted to have one. When Dawn told her about her epiphany of Lily being Lilith, Misty had thought, "How come she gets an epiphany, and I don't?" Now she thought she might have one.

"Whoever provides you food each day," she told the cat, "is your Master. If you provide your own food, you are your own Master." She smiled.

"If that's true," she confided in the cat, "I've been my own master since I was eleven."

The cat jumped off the bed and ran into the bathroom. A minute later, Nadia walked out of the bathroom and said, "I've been my own master since my mom died five years ago."

Other than the fact that she wouldn't let Misty leave, Nadia was cool. She helped Misty dye her hair green and polished her nails black. She brought heaps of food back to the room, most of which was good when you scraped the rotten parts away. She never dressed provocatively, but she seemed to exude sexuality.

"What's your story," Misty asked her, "How did you end up in a second-rate tourist attraction working for an evil witch?"

"I was born a naiad. About a mile west of here, there is a cave that leads to an underground spring. It was there that my mother met a satyr named Ralph. (At least, she *thinks* it was Ralph.) In a drunken orgy, I was conceived. I was brought up a child of Hedonism.

Last year, I ran away. I was sick of my parent's life of constant debauchery. I rebelled. There must be more to life than Sex, Drugs, and Rock & Roll. I wasn't prepared for life in the big city. I had never seen anything like Dickinson Dude Ranch. I hoped to get a job as an accountant or a dental hygienist, but there is surprisingly little work here. The only jobs available for folk like us is in the entertainment industry. I was auditioning for a role as one of the prostitutes who survived the alamo in a community college production of "It Wasn't All Bad".

Philippa seduced me with promises of paid holidays and health-care benefits. I became her familiar. I never imagined I'd end up kidnapping a nice girl like you and imprisoning her. I'm sorry."

"Why don't you quit?"

"When I ran away from home, I did not know that the squares hated us. (That's what we have always called them, although I understand they're known as 'muggles', now.) They hate all things magical. They would defenestrate all magic from the world if they could. My pride won't let me go home. I have to work for witches and leprechauns and such or starve.

Misty felt sorry for her and provided succor in the only way she knew how.

"Don't you dare change into a cat while I'm down here," she warned.

If Starr could have driven due east, she could have had the girls in Dickinson Dude Ranch in 10 minutes. She couldn't, though, because there were no roads. There were only deer trails. She had to drive them back out the north entrance to White-Tail Ranch, east on I-20 to Tyler, and south on SH 69. The exit to <u>Dickinson Dude Ranch</u> was plainly marked. Starr dropped them off at the entrance, paid for their admission and gave them $20.

The girls both liked Chloe and didn't need Starr's admonition to keep an eye on her.

"You keep an eye on Alys," Bonnie reposted.

"Yeah, keep an eye on her pussy," Connie howled, enormously amused by her own wit.

It took the girls less than half-an-hour to blow the money on rides and candy at the arcade.

"I'm still hungry," Connie complained.

"Use your doggie senses to find us some food," Bonnie suggested.

Connie and Nadia reached for the "Big Breakfast Box" at the same time. It looked as if it might have been thrown away unopened and unused. Connie growled. Nadia hissed.

The dumpster behind McDonald's had been Nadia's regular feeding ground for weeks now. She resented this newcomer intruding on her territory.

"There's live rats behind the diner," she suggested.

"Ate a bad rat, once," Connie replied, "got sick and died. Been off 'em ever since."

Reluctantly, they decided to share. When they opened it, they discovered the reason it had been thrown away was because a baby had thrown up on it as soon as it was opened.

"Still good as new except for the baby vomit," Connie said. Nadia shrugged. They ate it, but without relish.

"Could use a little relish," Connie joked, but Nadia was not amused.

When they were full, they got sleepy.

"You know any good sleeping places?" Connie asked. "I got a good place," Nadia said, "but I'm not supposed to tell anyone about it. Philippa's holding a girl prisoner there and nobody is supposed to know about it."

Bonnie joined the conversation. "What if we give this Philippa Connie as a fuck-toy?"

"Philippa isn't really into dirty, smelly slags with fleas…or ungroomed bushes for that matter. No offense, Connie."

"None taken, but what if we declare our loyalty to her?" Connie asked. "We could pretend to be her loyal subjects. Every wicked despot needs minions."

Philippa was pissed. When she had reported to Agatha and Mildred that Lily Inouye was the actual 'Lilith', they had laughed.

"All the more reason to stay away from her," they had said. A goddess is way above our paygrade. Just kill the kid, Chloe, as instructed. Most people associate her with the new matriarchal religion. Women all over the world will be outraged. Just make sure men are blamed."

They hung up and went back to what they had been doing; and Philippa knew what that was. Here she was out in the Texas heat, doing all the work, and they were at home watching *The Crucible*, drinking wine, and laughing their asses off. She unlocked the door of the hide-out and threw it open.

The first thing she saw was Connie and Misty wrestling around on the floor. She glared at Nadia, who was getting her toenails painted rainbow colors by Bonnie.

"What the hell is going on here?" she demanded.

Bonnie threw herself on the floor and did the whole 'bowing and scraping' shtick. She had seen it on *The Three Stooges* and knew the whole bit. You get down on your knees and fully extend your arms. Then you bow until your nose hits the floor. You say, "Salami, Salami". Then Curly looks at Larry and says, "Baloney!" It looks stupid, but Bonnie knew that egomaniacal mistresses love it.

"We ask that you allow us to stay, Mistress and be your humble servants. We are mere street urchins, but we have special skills. Connie is an expert tracker, and I am a trained assassin."

"I've already killed once," she could not help bragging.

Philippa found a chair and pulled it in close to the two girls, Nadia, and Bonnie.

"It just so happens," she said, "that I'm in need of a sacrifice. I must convince the Dark Lord to allow me my pursuit of Lily. The coven says that we are not going after her, but if the Dark Lord demands it, they will allow me to go after her. If you wish to serve me, sacrifice Misty. And while you're at it, get rid of the one with the hairy bush.

Nadia and Bonnie looked at each other. What their eyes telegraphed each other was, "This old bat is crazy." What they actually said was, "Yeah! Ok. Right. Sacrifice, sure. Sounds like a plan. Great!"

Chloe and Chris sat in a swan in the Tunnel of Love.

Chloe stopped Chris when he slipped his hand inside her bra.

"I promised Aunt Irene I wouldn't get pregnant until I was at least 30."

"Sweetie, you can't get pregnant from having your breast caressed."

"But isn't it like a slippery slope?"

"Relax, Chloe. You and I can give each other a lot of pleasure without anyone getting pregnant. You just have to trust me."

"Later they dozed off in each other's arms. They felt warm and relaxed and carefree. Suddenly, the tunnel reverberated with the sound of gunfire. Chloe heard her stepmother yelling, "Chloe, get off the ride before it comes out into the open again."

Once you have passed the EXIT sign you're outside where the passengers load and unload. Chloe could see the flaps up ahead.

"Chris, let's get out of here. The gunshots are coming from outside." They jumped out of the boat and splashed over to the side where the two plaster-of-Paris mermaids lounged languorously.

"I told you premarital sex was dangerous," Chloe whispered.

A figure waving a flashlight came into view three boats back. Chloe started to call out, but Chris clamped a hand over her mouth. "We better see who it is first."

They crawled behind the mermaids and held their breath. The figure in the boat stood as he passed them. He shined his flashlight on the mermaids and spotted the kids behind them.

"Aha," he said, and immediately cracked his head on a cupid who had darted out to shoot an imaginary arrow at the riders. He fell back in the boat and dropped the gun he had been holding into the water.

Chris waded out and retrieved the pistol. He brought it back to their hiding place.

"I wonder if these things work when they're wet," Chris pondered. Pointing the barrel away from them, he pulled the trigger.

It worked.

"AHH!" the figure in the boat cried. He had stood up in the boat again and the bullet that Chris had accidentally fired hit him right in the asshole. He was waving his arms and screaming as he passed through the plastic flaps of the EXIT.

There were multiple gunshots and a loud splash as the man was shot out of the boat.

"I hope I didn't kill that guy," Chris whispered, "I could get grounded for that."

CHAPTER SIXTEEN

DEATH IN THE PINEY WOODS

"He had a gun when he ran in there," Starr explained to the officer.

"We know he hired some thugs to commit mayhem," Dawn added.

"Although we thought it was Alys they were after rather than Chloe," Scout said.

"Shut up!" Lucky hissed.

"When he came out of the tunnel, he was all agitated and swinging his arms around and we assumed he was taking aim at us," Starr continued.

"When you assume," Officer Holcum observed, "you make an <u>ass</u> out of <u>u</u> and <u>me</u>." Officer Holcum had grown up in Tyler and much of his training had been listening to aphorisms from Police Chief Andy Hardy. He looked down at the body in the little artificial stream of the amusement park ride. The water downstream was no longer pink the way it had been when he arrived. The current kept banging the head against the dock, bang, bang, bang. Officer Holcum took off his hat and tried to think of some appropriate words to speak. He was interrupted by his sister, Betty Lou, who he had brought along because their parents had gone to church, and he didn't want to leave her at home by herself.

"How come there just happened to be four heavily armed women waiting for him when he come out?" she asked.

"We had an anonymous tip," Dawn said.

"If you're through questioning those kids," Scout said, indicating Chris and Chloe, "could I take them back to the motel?"

The ambulance driver had wrapped a towel around the wet kids, but still they shivered. Scout feared they were in shock.

"Yeah, go ahead," Betty Lou said, then she and Officer Holcum said at the same time: "Just don't leave town." Officer Holcum scowled at his little sister. That should have been HIS line.

"There were reports of gunfire before you all started up, is that right?" Officer Holcum asked, retaking control of his investigation.

"That's right," Starr said, "we heard gunfire inside the ride when we pulled up. We had already been warned that Chloe was in there. I hollered for her to stay hidden.

Betty Lou yelled at the spectators that had gathered round, "Did any of y'all see anybody going into the exit of the Tunnel of Love?"

"I seen the whole thing," a tubby little girl said to Betty Lou.

"Gol dang it, Vicky. Talk to me. I'm the officer in charge," Officer Holcum said.

"That guy," Vicky said, pointing at the corpse, "was running for his life. The red-headed woman was chasing after him and shooting at him."

"A red-haired woman," Officer Holcum said, taking his pocket notebook out of his pocket. He opened it up and licked his pencil. Did you notice any other relevant details?"

"Well, she was wearing a Texas A&M uniform."

"Hmm. Military-style dungarees," he wrote. Anything else?"

"No. That's about it. Oh, yeah, there was one other thing. Her nose was tied on to her face with a Texas A&M bandana."

Before the adults had shown up and ruined it, Chris and Chloe had managed to bring each other to orgasm without actually having intercourse.

As they followed Scout back to the motel, Chris whispered to Chloe, "I'll bet that wicked witch is half-way back to Seattle by now."

"So?"

"She's sure not going to return to her motel room."

"Yeah?"

"So, it's just sitting there, empty. With that big bed."

Chloe stopped. She did some processing. Then, she did some calculating. Either one of them could have been killed by a stray bullet. Adults were always fucking things up. You never know if this will be your last day alive.

"Do you have protection?" she asked.

Wynonna thought about the nosy parkers at the Alamo hotel who had interrupted her and the account manager when they were having sex. She thought it might be a hoot to sic Manny and Mo on them for revenge. Maybe these fellas would interrupt them at their moment of climax.

The folks that killed your boss are staying at the Alamo," she told them. "Why don't y'all pay them a little visit. Room 145. Tell 'em I said, "Hi."

As Chris finished for the second time, Chloe reached back and grabbed the headboard. Unfortunately, as she did her hand brushed against some green slime left from a previous sexual encounter. For a moment, Chloe's mind was filled with the Dark Side of sex. She saw how it could be used to manipulate and enslave people. She saw how money and power could pervert the holiest experience two people can share. Then she had an insight that she shared with Chris:

"Sex is intended as a participatory sport, not a spectator sport."

"Baseball is both," her brilliant lover replied.

"Do you want to go field some flies and grounders?"

"Sure. Let's go."

Mannie and Mo approached the door with guns drawn just as it was thrown open by Chris. He had a bat on his shoulder and Chloe had her hands full of baseballs and gloves.

Mannie pulled the trigger of his gun and sent a bullet hurling into the engine block of a 1998 Ford Escort. The blast from Mannie's gun frightened Mo and he shot his big toe off.

"HOMER!" he screamed.

The scream unnerved Mannie and his second shot blew out the light over the door of Room 144. He never had a chance for a third shot, because Chris had taken two steps forward and conked him over the head with a baseball bat.

Mo fell over the prostrate body of Manny and Chris and Chloe ran away.

There was police tape blocking rooms 145 and 146 when we returned to the motel. Scout and Lucky were in the parking area, breaking the news to Cathy about Stanley. The police assured us that the only victim was a guy who could only say 'Homer' who had been taken to the hospital in Tyler. Chloe and Chris, although missing, were assumed to be safe.

Starr invited me to her room for a drink.

"I think Dawn is right," Starr told me, "I think Lily is the reincarnation of Lilith. When we were at your cabin, Bonnie kept talking about how many men she would kill in the coming war, and chills ran down my spine when I heard Lily's response."

"There will be no killing," she said, "Not this time. The time of War is over. The battles will be fought in the halls of Academia. 'Soldiers', which are just soulless killing machines, will be replaced by scholars, philosophers, artists, and intelligent theologians."

Bonnie objected that that last one was an oxymoron, but Lily was on a roll.

"Every conflict, from the smallest border dispute to the grandest questions of Ideology, will be argued before the United Nations, and the decisions made there will be accepted as law. The appeals process will be open and ongoing."

"Yeah, that Lily can talk," I agreed, "but she's not a very good judge of character. Don't forget it was just a week ago that she was head over heels in love with Philippa."

"The kid's got a lot of growing up to do but there's something special about her."

"Yeah, that exotic Polynesian sex appeal."

"You tapping that?" Starr asked me with unnecessary crudity. I couldn't imagine what "tapping that" had to do with any sort of sexual intimacy, but I wasn't going to ask. Starr was obviously angry with me about something and couldn't wait to tell me the many ways she disapproved of my promiscuity. I changed the subject.

"Nan breathed her last breath onto Dawn's chest," I said, "I'm convinced her soul jumped into Dawn's body at that time."

"Don't talk crazy, Alys. Are you saying that Dawn's little squatty-body has two souls in it? Is she a split personality? One day chocolate is her favorite ice cream; the next day it's pistachio?"

"Split personalities are a real thing. There can be people with one dominant, and one more reclusive personality."

"Would they be aware of each other?"

"I don't think Dawn brings anything to the table. I think she just sits in the back seat and watches Nan navigate through life."

"Well, somebody in Dawn's body really likes Lily. You're saying it's Nan?"

"Nan loves me," I said, beginning to get a bit irritated. There were a lot of questions in life, a lot of things I don't understand, but one thing was sure; the love between Nan and me was inviolable and eternal. It's one of those sacred things that others question at their own peril.

"Well, it ain't Dawn! Dawn's in the back seat, remember? Looks to me like Nan's got a big old hard-on for Lily!"

I'm left-handed and it surprises a lot of people, even experienced fighters. They expect a feint with the left followed by a hard right. I caught Starr smack in the nose before she could put up a defense.

I heard the bone in her nose crack, and I saw the blood gushing uncontrollably.

She didn't fight back. It's really impossible to fight when you're blinded by your own blood. She pinched the flow of blood with her right hand and with her left she pulled up her T-shirt to stanch the flow of blood.

"A Picture is Worth a Thousand Words". The look that Starr gave me told me everything she felt about our relationship. I had lied, cheated, and broken her heart, and yet, after all these years, she had considered me her friend…until I had attacked her over the affection of a dead woman.

I knew what Judas Iscariot must have felt like when she turned and walked away. I knew the sickening remorse was with me to stay. I thought of the words of an Elton John song:

"Love lies bleeding in my hands."

CHAPTER SEVENTEEN

Cathy couldn't cope with the loss of Stanley. He had always been more than a brother to her, more than a lover. He had been like a twin, her other half. Without his strength, she was unable to face the real world. She fled to the fantasy world where she felt safest. She, once again, became Catherine of Aragon.

"We must flee," she told the waif who had stayed at the castle so often. In truth, she had grown fond of the little ragamuffin.

"I'm staying here with Chris," Chloe declared.

"It is no longer safe in our Kingdom. I fear even France might not be safe. Assassins abound! We must hie to Espana."

"You go ahead, Your Majesty. I'm staying."

Exasperated with the little guttersnipe's impertinence, the queen went out to the coach that waited outside the room of the Inn. As she entered the car, she noticed Scout, the nanny, sitting across from her.

As her astrologer closed the door firmly behind her, she cried out:

"Madame Aurora, what are you doing? Surely, you will not desert me, as well. I couldn't bear it."

"I'm sorry, Your Majesty. I see a bright future for you, but first, you need a rest. Scout will take good care of you, but my place is here, in the fight for Justice, Liberty, and Equality. (and Starr.)

Starr and Lucky stood side by side and waved good-by as the State Senator from the great state of Texas was sent off to a luxurious sanitarium in Madrid.

Nadia, Bonnie, Connie, and Misty stood at the mouth of a cave.

"You have to go with Nadia and Misty," Bonnie insisted.

Connie was crying. "I thought we were friends. I've never had a friend like you before. Not in ANY lifetime!"

"You are the best friend I've ever had, too, Connie. We'll be together soon, I promise; but for now, you have to stay with Nadia and Misty. You like to play with Misty, don't you?"

"Yes. I guess so. She, at least, understands the concept of 'Fetch'. But why can't I stay with you?"

"You are guileless, Connie. You can't lie. What's the first thing you would say to Phillipa when we got back?"

"Hi, Philippa, we killed Nadia and Misty and we didn't hide them in a cave."

"You see the problem, don't you, honey?"

A distant gunshot brought home the perilous conditions the girls had found themselves in.

"We can't stand here talking, Connie. Nadia forgot to tell us that the entrance to her hidden home is in the middle of a huge deer preserve. There are hunters out here with everything from bows and arrows to high-powered rifles. They all want to carry a carcass home on their hood. They are trigger-happy and itching to kill something. Go on now. Just hide in the cave until I return for you."

Connie put her hands on Bonnie's shoulders and licked her face. Then, with Misty, she entered the cave. Nadia lingered behind and said, "I guess you'll really miss your friend."

Gruffly, Bonnie said, "She ain't nothing but a hound dog and she ain't no friend of mine."[5]

A shot-off toe will bleed like a stuck pig. Mo had to be taken to the Emergency Room in Tyler. All Chief-of-Security, Earnest Lee Symple,

---

[5] The King

could tell Starr and Lucky was that his accomplice might be named 'Homer'.

"That's all we could get him to say," he told them.

"I think we are going to have to find Chloe on our own," Starr told Lucky.

"Ya think?"

"Hey, don't be such a smart-ass. When I first met you, you were trying to convince little old ladies that you could communicate with their dead cats. "Little Poopsy misses you very much in the afterlife. Wishes you were there,"

"Yeah, when I first met you, you didn't believe a fist would fit in…"

"OK. I guess I didn't think that one all the way through. I mean, if a ten-pound baby will come OUT of there, it shouldn't be so hard…"

"We did have some good times, though."

"Yeah, it's not your fault that I had Alys Loxley to compare you to."

It was a serious point of contention between these two that Starr had made love to the Legendary Lesbian Lothario, and Lucky had not.

"Speaking of fantastic sexual partners, you know who I miss? I miss Dawn. Where is Dawn, now? I've lost track of her."

"You just saw her last week, Grandma. Remember? She was bowing and scraping to Lily, like she was some kind of god, or something. *Tres embarrassing!*

She was convinced to go back to Fort Worth and join the FWPD where she is making great strides in solving the Hecate Collins murder. She has concluded that <u>you</u> must have done it."

"I…But, WHAT?"

Just kidding.

Dawn showed the FWPD how Philippa framed you. You are in the clear. Dawn is in hot pursuit of Philippa."

"Didn't that little 'Misty' girl spot Philippa in the Dude Ranch, recently?"

"Starr, you are hopelessly behind on the plot. Why don't we go somewhere private, and I'll fill you in on all the latest twists and turns?"

"You're reading my mind, oh Crystal-Ball gazer."

"Yeah. And I don't like the part about the fist."

"How many bullets does he have left?" Chris asked Chloe as they ran down the Main Street of Dickinson's Dude Ranch.

"How the hell should I know?"

"He shot twice at the motel. He probably has four bullets left."

"How do you figure?" Chloe asked, dodging a tourist with a camera.

"Every cowboy show I've ever seen, the bad guys carry six-shooters."

"I hope the guy shooting at us saw the same movies." Chloe saw Starr and Lucky across the street. "I've got to talk to them," she said, breathlessly, "Let's split up. You run to the west exit. When you get there, turn right and head into the forest. I'll catch up. Got it?"

A streetlamp exploded twenty feet over their heads.

"Three left!" Chris shouted and took off running.

"Lucky he's a lousy shot," Chloe thought, as she crossed the street to Starr and Lucky.

"Help," she pleaded, "There's a guy chasing us. He has a gun. And he looks exactly like Marty Feldman." Then she ran off.

"Who's Marty Feldman?" Starr asked.

"You know. The googly-eyed guy in the Mel Brook's movies."

"There is a cross-eyed guy over there with a smoking gun in his hand."

"That could be him. Let's nab the little bastard."

Seeing two determined-looking women coming towards him, Mannie decided to run and hide. Nocturnal rodent that he basically was, he avoided confrontation. He ran down a back alley, then another. When he came to a dead end, he banged on the nearest door with his gun.

"Open up," he demanded, "Or I'll…"

He looked around and saw a nearby cat investigating a trashcan. "…I'll kill your cat!"

Phillipa opened the door. "Oh, please, sir. Don't kill my cat." With a smile, she let him in.

———⊰⊱———

Chloe wished she had thought to bring some water. When she had left the Dude Ranch, she had turned to her right and headed for the distant trees. She had passed miles of nothing but cactus and sagebrush. The trees were still a good way off. She wondered why she hadn't caught up with Chris, yet. She was sure she had told him to turn right once out the gate.

She wiped sweat off her forehead and laughed at the memory of Aunt Irene's story about "The Light". Her Buddhist studies had taught her that, upon death, one should always "follow the light". The Light would lead one out of the Karmic Wheel of repeated reincarnation into the bliss of unified energy that is non-being. When she got hit by a car, Irene had found herself in a dark tunnel with a bright light at the end. "Come," the Light called.

"I got confused," she explained later. "I followed the shadows"

She later confessed there was nothing 'accidental' about it. I wasn't through with life," she giggled.

Chloe wondered what made her think about that story. Was her subconscious telling her that Chris might have turned the wrong way 'accidentally'? "I'm sure I told him to turn right," she thought. "Or maybe I'm confused. I don't know. I'm hot. I'm tired. I can't think about it.

Chloe began obsessively rehashing her relationship with Chris. She wasn't sure it was "true love forever", but she couldn't imagine anyone better to lose her virginity to. Chris was sweet, and smart, and (let's face it) cute. She wasn't sure that Chris would always be in her life. There was only one thing she was really sure of. She imagined it in her head for the 100th time:

She's standing in front of a sold-out crowd at Ranger's Ballpark in Arlington, Texas. She tips her cap to the adoring fans. They cheer wildly.

The PA announcer says: Ladies and Gentlemen, let's hear it for the first woman to hit .300 in a season. MS CHLOE DUNNALLY-williams".

She would hold her hands out graciously to the crowd and accept their adoration. Then she would single out her stepmother in the crowd. The old bitch would be sitting with one of her hippy-dippy girlfriends, half her age. Chloe would do an elaborate wind up and come over the top with a BOING! BIG OL MIDDLE FINGER! "UP YOURS, STARR!

That was her fate. She knew it. She never doubted it for a second.

Chloe was dead-tired by the time she reached the tree line. She'd had no hydration in over eight hours. As she sat in the shade of the first tree she came to; it did not surprise her all that much when she was visited by her Fairy Godmother.

She was, however, somewhat taken aback to see that her F.G.M. had chosen to appear in the form of a Knight Without Shining Armor named Matt.

Chloe laughed derisively as Matt tried to floss the gap between his front teeth with a blade of grass.

"Hayseed," she chided.

"Did you just call me a hayseed?" Matt asked.

"Yes."

"Why?"

"It seemed applicable. Besides, I may never get the chance to call someone a hayseed again."

"Makes sense. But, you know, you really ought to look for the positive in new people when you meet them. It's the best policy all around, besides the nicest. The world could stand being a bit nicer, couldn't it?"

Chloe was dizzy and having trouble following Matt's reasoning.

"For instance," he continued, "what's good about a hayseed?" (Long Pause)

"That's right, he knows the countryside. For example, if you ask a hayseed where the nearest water is, he might be able to tell you that there is some delicious, refreshing water just two hundred yards due west of where you sit."

Chloe struggled to her feet. "I want you to know, sir, that I'm not interested in a thing you say. Your low-brow buffoonery holds no interest for me at all. I just happen to feel like taking a walk. If you would be so good as to point the way west…"

Matt pointed. Chloe dreamily laid her head on the knight's bicep and sighted down his arm like the barrel of a gun. His fingers pointed to a gap between two trees not far away. Chloe staggered that way.

"There appears to be a path," she said through parched lips.

"It's a deer path, my lady. Let the Deer guide you."

Any question as to whether this was real or a dream, was removed when Chloe came to a place where the deer path was completely covered by deer pellets. She held out her arm. This is the point in the story where the handsome, young knight takes the damsel's arm and leads her around any unpleasantness. Chloe was sadly disappointed to find that her knight had deserted her.

"It's too bad, really," she thought, "his bicep was quite firm. I would have liked to use it for a pillow, tonight."

"Besides," she continued, although several minutes of silence had gone by, "I thought he would ask me a lot of penetrating questions about myself that would lead to some sort of epiphany. Something like:

"Why do you suppose your stepmother so much?"

HA. I wish he HAD asked me that.

"Do you suppose it's fun having a notorious queer for a stepmother when you are growing up?" I would have answered. "Well, just try it, buster! Try going to school and having kids say, "Your mom's a carpet-muncher." How would you like that? I couldn't imagine what a 'carpet-muncher' was unless it was a new kind of vacuum cleaner."

Chloe began weeping copiously. Suddenly, Matt reappeared, peeking out from behind a Pine tree.

"Don't cry, Chloe. You're not even halfway to the pond and you're wasting hydration."

The field mouse scampering alongside of her offered no sympathy.

"You're right," she admitted to the tiny creature, "adopting my fellow man's stupidity as my own was stupid, but I was just a child and

I blamed her. I thought she did it to piss people off. I thought she was being provocative to hurt me.

Something about the way the mouse was looking at her made her think, "Unless there was a deeper reason why I hated my stepmother and was just using the prevailing prejudices of the time to cloak my true antipathy."

"That's quite a mouthful for a 15-year-old," Chip said to Dale, as she passed under their branch.

"He-He-He. Next, she'll be speaking in tongues," Dale chattered.

"Hey," Chip called out to her, "watch out for that fallen branch in front of…Oops!"

The damn chipmunks were still laughing and dancing and chattering when her face hit the mud. "Those revolting rodents, I'd like to…" Wait a minute. Mud?

She looked up and saw the pond ten feet in front of her. She hoped it was real. She dragged herself to the edge of the pond and found it was full of the Elixir of the Gods. Pure, clean water!

Chloe wasn't sure if the susurration that woke her was the wind in the grass or the deer communicating among themselves. One thing was sure. She was right dag-nab in the middle of a herd of deer. If the deer *were* communicating, they were doing it sub-vocally, or so quietly, one had to strain to hear anything.

One must WANT to hear them," Chloe thought to herself. She thought about all the radio and Sunday morning 'talk' shows where the most convincing "opinions" were the ones spoken the loudest. The soft murmur was relaxing, and Chloe found it easy to think. She searched for her earliest memory.

The earliest one was writing her name in the sandbox at Worthinghampton Orphanage. Eirene (Chloe always thought of her with an "E" on the front of her name) had been trying earlier to teach her to spell, but it was all mumbo-jumbo to Chloe then.

Now, she looked at the letters C-H-L-O-E, and thought, "That's me." She had been four, then.

"I don't remember anything else about my early childhood," she told the hummingbird that was hovering before her. Chloe was no longer hallucinating. She was rested and hydrated. She was a bit hungry, but she knew the hummingbird was just a bird. She felt, though, that the fact that the hummingbird was hanging around despite the lack of any sugar source, was enough justification to talk to it.

Besides, it was a good listener.

"I remember going to church when I was five and thinking what a good goof it was for the fat man in the white suit behind the pulpit. He was pulling the strings of a hundred people. He could make them laugh or cry.

"Make them jump on one foot," I encouraged, telepathically.

It was hard work for Reverend Swamp. He was constantly dabbing sweat off his forehead. By the time the ushers passed around the 'offering plates', his shirt was stained at the underarms with huge circles of perspiration.

It wasn't hard at all for me. I started out practicing alone in my room. The hard part was the words. I didn't know a lot of words, then. I knew that the whole point was to convince them that they **must** put some money in the tray. Brother Swamp would promise them Heaven if they did; and Hell if they did not. So, I started out promising candy if they would stand on one foot, and demerits if they didn't. When I took my act out on the playground, it didn't work. I discovered that if a kid stood on one foot, they expected their candy **right then**. Promises weren't enough. And nobody gave a shit about demerits.

I listened carefully in church, and I honed my act. You just have to remember to tell them that they will get everything you promise, AFTER THEY'RE DEAD!

I know, but, trust me, they'll buy it.

The hummingbird got bored and flew away. Chloe was still hungry. She thought about the conversation she overheard between Starr and Lucky when she was younger.

"Lilith is the best kept secret in Patriarchal history," Lucky told Starr.

They were talking in bed. Chloe was eavesdropping, not because there was anything she didn't already know about sex (both hetero and homo), but because they often had interesting conversations after sex, like her stepmother meeting Lucky when she was out on a date with Cathy. That kind of thing.

"Suddenly, she's starting to find relevance," Lucky said, "It's the 'Perfect Storm' of Feminism, the Death of God, and instant worldwide communication. It's no more than an old Creation myth found in the Dead Sea Scrolls. What's earth-shaking about it now is the idea that God made Man and Woman equals!

In the *Alphabet of Ben Sira,* God creates Adam and LILITH with the same clay. Do you remember how Eve was created?"

"From Adam's Rib!" Chloe crowed silently from her hiding place outside the door, but Starr couldn't guess.

"I might have fallen asleep when that sermon was preached," she said.

"God broke a rib off Adam and made woman," Lucky confirmed, "That makes us derivative, do you see? Second class citizens."

"After that day," Chloe said out loud to no one in particular, "I began to talk more about Lilith in my sermons. Eirene and Aggie still wrote most of my stuff, but I began to go off- script.   I was beginning to have my own ideas about how to make that crowd hop on one foot."

About mid-morning, the herd began to move. A week ago, or even yesterday, Chloe might have cynically assumed that somewhere out there an Alpha Male had decided it was time to move on and the herd simply followed. Now, she considered that it might be like a flock of birds that all decide at the exact same time to shift to the right or flow to the left. Perhaps, in this perfectly harmonious society, the herd had decided as one.

Chloe decided to follow along. It was mostly because of hunger. She hoped they would lead her to berries or fruit that would keep her alive. But it was also because she liked their quiet, peaceful lifestyle. She envied their calm acceptance that they were exactly where they were supposed to be in the universe. So, as they moved slowly northward, she followed along.

"Can anyone explain the point of pine trees to me?" she mused. "I mean, if you find yourself in an apple orchard in the summer, you're going to find food everywhere. There are apples in the trees, apples on the ground. But, in the Piney Woods of East Texas, you find nothing but pinecones. The deer eat them if there's nothing else, but I couldn't, no matter how I tried. They are nothing but bark."

The deer did reveal some berries, but it would have taken a whole bucketful to fill her stomach. When the herd found some mushrooms, she watched, curiously, as they ate them. None of the deer who ate the mushrooms freaked out or had orgies or anything, so she ate some of them, too. Either the schrooms or the full tummy made her reflective. She thought about the time she was famous as the harbinger of Lilith. People began to associate her with Lilith. Some even speculated that she WAS Lilith.

She was glad when the sun began to set, and the deer decided to stop for the night. She found herself a comfortable spot under a tree and fell immediately asleep. It was a restless sleep, however, and she could hear the owls asking "Who? Who?"

They blended in with her dream of a quest to find Lilith.

"Who is Lilith?" she asked.

She asked Brother Swamp and he told her, "She is a demon who was cast out of Eden because she insisted on being on top. She enjoyed sex shamelessly and wore poor Adam out. Then she fornicated with the serpent and the wild creatures of the jungle." As he told her this, there was a bulge in his trousers.

"Who is Lilith?" she asked Cathy.

"I am Lilith," she answered. "I am the Queen of women. It is my Destiny to rule women and cast men into slavery, as they enslaved us for 2000 years."

"You are Lilith," Chris told me, but he had a bulge in his trousers as well, and she suspected he was just being nice.

"Lilith," Alys informed me, "is the only famous female I haven't nailed…yet."

She was tossing and turning when Matt lay down next to her. He put his arm under her head. His bicep was amazingly comfortable.

"Learn from the herd," he whispered in her ear.

"Matt, sweetie, why are you whispering inane rhymes into my ear?"

"Learn from the herd," he repeated, "The Deer" is not one deer. "The Deer" are many. Lilith is not one person".

Chloe slept after that. When she awoke the next morning, the deer were gone... except for one stag. His antlers were large. The muscles in his upper legs bulged. She walked next to him until they came to a clearing.

In the middle of the clearing was a small cabin. Even from fifty yards away, the sound of Lynyrd Skynyrd could be heard blaring from the cabin. Alys Loxley was dancing blissfully around the back porch with a bottle of Jack Daniel's in her hand. She was singing loudly and off-key.

"LORD KNOWS I CAN'T CHANGE. LORD HELP ME I CAN'T CHA-A-A-NGE." She picked up a broom and began to play air-guitar, drunkenly.

Chloe had reached her Destination. She was home.

CHAPTER EIGHTEEN

MERE ANARCHY

Philippa had managed to get one of the apartments where employees of the Dude Ranch lived. They ran along the back alleys where tourists never wandered.

She let Manny in through the kitchen door and peeked out the window. She saw Starr and Lucky come running up and looking around for their quarry. She recognized Starr.

"Why is a world-class assassin after you?" she asked.

"We may have accidentally shot at her stepdaughter…"

"We?"

"Yeah, me and Mo, but Mo shot his toe off."

"Well, you're safe, now. Come on in the living room."

When they entered the living room, Manny stopped abruptly. "What the fuck?"

Tied to chair in the center of the room was Chris Hanlon.

When her john was through, Sally took the $300 off the dresser and went outside the building. She found both the reception and the privacy were better outside. The voice on the other end of the line said, "Speak."

"Phillipa, it's Sally, at the 19th Hole. I'm pretty sure I recognized the guy I was with just now. I seen him when I was in Chicago. His wallet says he's 'Harry Graves', but he was known as Chuck 'Bent Nose'

Benton when I was there. He's a well-known hitman. He's packing heat."

"Did he give you any idea what he's in town for?"

"He's asking about a cabin that supposed to be close by, and someone called Alice Longley, or something like that."

"He say anything about a 'Chloe' or a 'Lily'?"

"Nah, just that Alice."

"Thanks, I won't forget you…um, Sally."

Philippa was alone in her bedroom, and, with nothing else to do, she was getting drunk. She thought about her unique life. "They should make a movie about it," She imagined telling the ghost-writer for the hundredth time:

"My momma was a whore in St. Louis Mo. I fell in love with my stepdaddy when I was thirteen. We robbed a string of liquor stores together; had a real swell time.

Then the son-of-a-bitch drove off and left me standing outside the liquor store with a smoking .32 in one hand and a bag of banknotes in the other. I did hard time and was forced into the wicked ways of homosexuality. I developed a taste for it over the 10 years I was inside, but I discovered something else while I was there: the Wicca Sisterhood.

I worked my way up the ranks, past the tree-huggers and midnight dirty dancers. I was initiated into Real witchcraft by Agatha and Mildred, two of the meanest old witches you'll ever see. We mixed up some strange brews in our big ol' boiling pot over the years. Had some weird visions.

Then I heard about Lilith; how she was going to take over the world and get rid of all those bastards like J.D., who ran off and left me holding the bag…literally!"

Then, one night, we threw some peyote in that big, black cauldron and I had a vision of how I would become famous! I would kill Lilith! I would be as famous as John Wilkes Booth!

Then, the camera would slowly back away from me standing there over the dead body of Lilith saying something like, "Fuck All Tyrants!"

Philippa played the movie over in her mind. At her trial, the judge would condemn her to be burnt at the stake, but the mob would rush into the courtroom yelling, "Philippa, Philippa!"

"Philippa! Open the door."

Philippa walked into the kitchen and opened the back door. The girl named Bonnie walked in and threw a bloody knife on the kitchen floor.

"It's done."

"Where's Nadia?"

"I'm sorry, ma'am. She fell in love with Misty. She tried to interfere. I had no choice."

"Well, fuck me running. You killed my familiar! Damn. I was really looking forward to curling up with a little pussy tonight. Oh, well."

She began to eye Bonnie speculatively.

"Try it," Bonnie thought, "and you'll be #2 on my list."

Her first murder had not happened like she planned. She remembered all those nights she had spent feeling sorry for herself when her stepfather was through with her. She remembered calmly listing every person who had ever belittled or disrespected her. When the list was completed, she would dream of starting at the bottom and working her way up. When she got back up to #1, she would look at her stepfather's terrified face and say, "Hasta la vista, Motherfucker!"

She hadn't even known Jake. She knew he had attempted to rape Connie. That was enough. She was oddly unconcerned about his death. He had been a bad man who had gotten what he deserved.

It just wouldn't go away. She kept seeing his face pucker like a prune. The blood spray. The brain matter. Pieces of skull bouncing off the wall. Like the tune you can't get out of your head, it kept replaying in Bonnie's mind.

"You did good, kid," Philippa assured her, "Now listen to my plan: I've kidnapped the boyfriend. I've got him tied up in the living room. I'm going to tell Lily he's here and she has to come alone to save him. Then, I'll kill him right in front of her and then, kill her too. What do you think? Pretty diabolical, huh?"

"Why would Lily care what you do to Chris?"

"He's her boyfriend, isn't he?"

"Lily doesn't have a boyfriend. In order for your plan to work, you would have had to kidnap Scout. That's who Lily was all into…before she met you."

"Well, shit."

At that very moment, Nadia (very much alive) was reentering the deep recesses of the underground dwelling of her people. She had been terribly homesick when she'd been on the surface where people were so bored, they had to make up plays about old battles and reenact them for tourists who were so bored they would travel 500 miles to spend three months' salary to spend a week in a stupid tourist trap watching a stupid reenactment of the slaughter of a bunch of guys who had been so bored they had gotten involved in a territorial dispute that had nothing to do with them.

Things were much simpler by the underground pool. So were sentences.

Nadia could not stand another day with Connie and Misty. When they weren't wrestling around doing who knows what to each other, they were talking.

Misty would talk about the time the band forgot her and left her in Roswell, New Mexico. "I was kidnapped by illegal aliens," she told Connie. "A family of illegals from Mexico tried to take me home with them. The coyote tried to anally probe me. Fortunately, I was rescued by Martians."

Connie would go on for hours about her lifetimes as dogs.

"Once this old hound dog got stuck in me when we were mating. We were doing it in the alley when a bunch of human kids came up on us and scared poor old Rascal. The more they laughed and hollered, the more stuck Rascal got. It hurt like a bitch."

Nadia finally just got fed up and left them there on the surface.

"Y'all stay here in the cave until Bonnie comes back for you. Remember, no chasing rabbits and don't eat anything you find around that meth lab.

Virgil dialed the number three times before he got it right. Since Stanley Scovall had been killed, Virgil didn't know who he was working for. He suspected it was the billionaire, J.R. Johnson, but nothing had ever been spelled out.

"This here is J.R. Johnson. What'cha got for me?"

"Sir, things are beginning to get a little out of hand."

"Say no more. You've said too much already."

"But, sir, the thing is…"

"HA! Just Kidding. Talk all you want to. We got nothing to hide, right? At least, I don't. I just found out I have terminal cancer. I've got six months, tops. I, literally, can't spend the money fast enough. So, I don't care what happens, now.

The lesbians can take over, now, for all I care. Well, it's been good talking to you, kid. I'm proud of the job you've done as a public servant in Fort Worth. You ran those gay libbers out of town on a rail, shut down their commie school, and sent a bunch of kids back to their Christian parents where they belong.

"Keep up the good work, son, and you'll be Mayor before you know it. You've learned to suck up to rich and powerful people and that will take you far. The only other thing you need to learn is that monomaniacal Super-Villains get old and die, too.

Remember, if anyone asks, we never had this conversation. Just nod your head, if you understand, boy. Just nod your head. HA!"

"Hello Chuck. Or, would you prefer, 'Bent Nose'?"

"Don't say my name, you idiot. Listen, the job you originally offered me involved an isolated, old broad, without a witness within five miles. Now, I find freaking Starr Williams in the same motel as me, looking for the Preacher kid. Starr Williams is a stone-cold killer. I ain't doing it. Not alone. Not for the amount we agreed on.

"Alright. Alright. Don't get your panties in a bunch. I'll send the Dinkwater Gang out there to help you."

Virgil Wilder didn't mention that the last job the Dinkwater Gang was given was the kidnapping of Irene Worthinghampton; and that they had mistakenly kidnapped Aggie Goodman instead.

Upon hearing that the Dinkwater gang was on the way, Philippa was filled with concern. "One positive thing," she thought, "is they're not on our side. But if there was ever a gang that couldn't shoot straight, it was this bunch of fuckups.

She felt she ought to let Agatha and Mildred in on this new development. She considered the various incantations and spells she would need to conjure them and then said, "Fuck it," and just called them.

"Hey, Phil," Mildred said upon answering, "We've been watching *The Crucible* again. It's as funny as ever. Agatha had to make a zinfandel run, but as soon as she gets back, we're going to watch *The Salem Witch Trials*. I think its Kirstie Alley's greatest work."

"Except perhaps for her work on <u>Cheers</u>."

"I was talking about her contribution to witchcraft."

"So was I."

The two witches cackled their hilarity.

"Anyway, the thing is, Millie, things are escalating out here on the front. Battle lines are being drawn. Nobody's right, if everybody's wrong. Young people…"

"Phil! STOP. Zip it."

"Sorry, but do you think you and Agatha could come out here and help me. The three of us could rain down such destruction. It would be just like the good old days."

"That's a hard 'NO', kid. Now that there is so much more room on the bed, Ag and I are working on some new positions. For a 300-year-old, that Agatha's got some amazing moves."

"HEY! That's not fair."

"I'll tell you what. There's this coven out of Portland that's gone all ga-ga about Lilith. I'll send you the whole damn coven. There's about eight of them."

"Will they help me kill Lilith?"

"No, you dumb fuck, they worship Her. They will protect you from men, though. They will also help you get the job done on the kid. Just stay on mission.

Listen, I gotta go. I hear Agatha at the door. See ya."

When she was sure she had Philippa's attention, the caller said, "Lily is in a small cabin five miles south of the 19th Hole. There is only one road. You can't miss it." Then Scout hung up the phone and caught her flight to Madrid.

CHAPTER NINETEEN

FEAR, REGRET, AND DUBIOUS ENTERPRISE

Chris was frightened, at first, when the girl walked in and dropped the bloody knife on the floor. His fright increased when the girl and the woman began to discuss, quite openly, at least one murder. His hands were tied, so he couldn't cover his ears, but he did sing "When Johnny Comes Marching Home" loudly and was saying, "la- la- la- la, I can't hear anything" whenever he forgot the words. If he were completely honest, he would admit that he peed himself a little bit when Phillipa sneered at him and said, "If I were going to let you live, you'd be blindfolded."

He calmed down a little when the witch went to answer the phone and Bonnie leaned over and whispered, "Don't worry. I'm going to get us out of this alive."

He couldn't help noticing she wore no bra. He almost saw a nipple. The instinct for survival notwithstanding, Chris was a teenage male.

"What's your name?" he whispered, trying to get her to lean in close again.

Bonnie saw Philippa returning and slapped Chris hard. "WHERE IS SHE?" she demanded, "TELL ME RIGHT NOW!"

"It's OK, hon," Philippa called from the doorway, "I know where she is. We won't need him, anymore. Go ahead and take him out and kill him. Make sure the body is never found."

"Philippa?"

"Yes?"

"Could I keep him for one night?"

"What for?"

Bonnie blushed.

"Oh, I get it. You want to play with him before you throw him away. Sure, fine. You can keep him until the Wicca coven gets here. We can't do anything until then. Mind you, you take care of him, yourself. I'm not cleaning up any of his messes.

Dawn sat in the *Cattleman's* on Camp Bowie with her fiancé. Things were different there since the last time she had been. The two women across from them were obviously lovers and made no effort to hide it. Nan and Alys would not have ever been so bold when they were together. Everyone would have been scandalized. They might have been asked to leave.

Ever since Dawn had held Nan in her arms and watched her die, Dawn would address Nan when she talked to herself. Everybody talks to themselves now and then; Dawn would just address herself as 'Nan'.

"How did people live under such oppression just a couple of decades ago?" she wondered. There had been so many rules: whites couldn't love blacks, boys couldn't love boys, strong men couldn't love poetry, and girls couldn't love being in charge. The Beatles even wrote a song about it: "You Have to Hide Your Love Away".

Of course, they did. The Beatles saw everything, knew everything, had an answer for everything. Were they responsible for the way the world had changed? Maybe, partially. But the real heroes were the rebels who would not sacrifice their love at any cost. Despite the threats of ostracism, bullying, beatings, lynching's, being dragged by a car with chains, being kicked out of their homes, spat on, and all the rest; they refused to stop loving.

Those who went along with the fascist's rules sat in chain restaurants opposite their indifferent, insignificant other and dreaded each remaining moment of their life.

Dawn had her rebellion. Fueled by drugs, booze, and lust for a blue-haired Irish girl, she had made the Search for Lily her religion. That rebellion was crushed, in the most embarrassing and humiliating way, when Lily had told her, basically, to "Man Up!"

Like someone who has lost their religion, her pendulum swung way out the other way. She became a zealous materialist. She joined the Police Force and quickly proved that Hecate Collins had been murdered by Philippa Borgia. She made up with George Colter (He loved having her blow him in full uniform) and settled down to a life in the straight community.

It was only when he was through fucking her and lay there snoring, that she thought about the days with Starr, Lily, and the little girl, Misty, who said, "You can worship her, just don't love her."

John Dinkwater hated out-of-town jobs. He had been up and down just about every street in Ft. Worth (mostly while being chased by cops) and he thought that gave him, well, a home field advantage. His best friend and partner-in-crime, Andy Karp, reminded him they were being paid $300,000 for this out-of-town caper.

"That's $100,000 each," he said, rubbing his hands together.

"Besides," Stan March, the driver, said, "Tyler is such a small town, you couldn't get turned around or trapped, or anything."

John's little sister, Donna, was sitting in the back seat with her arms crossed, gritting her teeth. She uncrossed her arms and held an index finger in the direction of the driver, Stan.

"In the first place," she said, "We are never getting inside the Tyler City Limits. In the second place," she said, holding up the next digit over in front of Andy Karp's face, "$300,000 divided four ways is $75,000 each."

None of the guys were happy having Donna along, but Virgil Wilder insisted. The last time the gang had worked for Virgil (and Stanley Scovall), they had kidnapped the wrong girl.

The only one who had even noticed was Donna. Virgil said he wouldn't work with them again if Donna wasn't in charge. John was embarrassed to have his little sister in charge, but he needed the money.

Virgil had told them that it was a simple kidnapping for ransom job. In fact, they were a mere diversionary tactic to divert Starr's attention while an assassin from Chicago took care of Alys. If Starr didn't take out the whole gang, Virgil would have Chuck "Bent Nose" Benton kill the survivors and then he'd give "Bent Nose" their $300,000. Virgil had covered all the angles.

"What," he asked himself, "could possibly go wrong?"

Anne got a call from her boss, Mr. Worthinghampton.

"Listen, I just got off the phone with my sister, Celeste. For once, we agree with each other. She and I are in complete agreement that the schism between the women's churches must be exploited and encouraged. They must not be allowed to unite. Don't you agree?"

"Completely. Anyone should be allowed to worship any god they choose, but a disruption of the power structure is a different thing. It could cause chaos and anarchy.

"Excellent. It's good to hear a woman with a solid head on her shoulders. No emotional, menstrual rants from you, eh, baby?"

"I know my place in the order of things."

"Have you persuaded Alys, yet?"

"Oh, yes sir. We have discussed the situation and we are in complete agreement: The Wiccan faction is too militant and must be illuminated."

"Anne, did you just say 'illuminated'?"

"Negatory, sir. I said 'eliminated'."

"Good girl."

Celeste Worthinghampton and Zsa Zsa Bosnia looked like avenging angels in their white robes and scowling faces. They looked down on Agatha and Mildred, both literally and figuratively, from the dais of the Dianic Wiccan Church in Austin.

"So, we just found out that while you two were spending everyday scissoring and watching old Ally Sheedy movies…"

"Kirsty Alley."

The silence hung heavy in the air.

"Sorry."

"… your sister, Philippa, has gone completely off the reservation, and is planning to kill some kid named Lily. Is that correct?"

"She saw the girl transform into a dragon. She swears it is the goddess Lilith.

"Get this straight, ladies. What people see, don't mean shit. If some farm girl sees a vision, it doesn't become the Virgin Mary until the Pope <u>says</u> so. In this case, whatever Philippa saw wasn't a goddess until WE say it was.

"Right now, we don't need a goddess, we need a martyr. We need a sweet little girl who's preaching the gospel of Lilith to be assassinated by an ugly, brutal man. Then, we need you two and your sister swooping in and arresting this monster so we can put him on trial. We'll have the Trial of the Millennium. We'll put the Patriarchy itself on trial."

Chris lay shivering on the bed. He was shivering because he was naked, but he was also shivering because he knew he was about to get raped by a knife-wielding murderer.

Bonnie sat on the bed and began to undress. She was humming the theme song to "Rocky". She put on the shirt she slept in and got into bed. She had swiped the t-shirt from Alys Loxley; it had a blood-drenched peace sign on it.

"Does that symbol mean something?" Chris asked.

"To me it means the Peace Movement of the 1960's failed because it was pacifist. Those kids just sat there while the fascists used violence, and overwhelming force to convince the Silent Majority of their lies. That's how we ended up with Cheney and his sidekick Bush.

That's just me, of course. It's Alys's shirt. She told me she wore it to remind herself that, no matter how noble the cause, innocent blood is always spilt."

"Listen," Chris said, "I'll try to cooperate, but I don't know if I can get it up under duress."

"What the fuck are you talking about? I'm trying to keep you alive."

"You aren't going to rape me?"

"Don't sound so disappointed. You're lucky. You're in bed with the one female hetero in Texas who wouldn't enjoy having sex with you. I'm like one of those Arab girls who's had her clit removed. I'd rather have an appendix removed than have sex. I just think Chloe is cool, so I'm helping you."

"So, what's the plan?"

"Well, that's the problem. I don't actually have a plan. The only thing I can tell you is: 'Be ready. If you see a chance, take off running. Don't worry about me. The witch likes me. If you weren't around, she'd try to get me in bed, and I'd have to kill her."

"You sound like a Lilitian."

"What's a Lilitian?"

"A member of the Church of Lilith. It's a brand-new religion started up by Alys Loxley and my girlfriend, Chloe. Lilithians don't believe in turning the other cheek. They believe the punishment for attempted rape is instant death. No arrest. No trial. No jury. Just instant death.

Mom and dad say I'm not allowed to date a Lilithian. I wonder what they would think if they knew I was dating one of the Founders?"

CHAPTER TWENTY

ODE ON A DISTANT PROSPECT OF ETON COLLEGE

There were five of us in the little shack now. Five women and one bathroom.

Lucky is here because Starr is, and Starr is here…well, I don't know why Starr is here. Maybe she thinks she'll find a Good Fight. Chloe is here because she's convinced that I'm Lilith. She doesn't see that I'm just Auntie Alys. Lily is obviously here to make the rest of us feel inferior.

Lucky is like a younger, smarter, more ambitious version of Starr. They both have an aura of flamboyance and derring-do that makes boys dislike them and girls develop big, old crushes on them. The difference between them is that Starr never gave a thought to who she was or where she was going. She lives in the <u>NOW</u>. Lucky has been driven her whole life to be something *(anything!)* other than Mabel Bett's daughter. She always has an angle. She always has a scheme. She always has a plan.

Starr is the strongest, most courageous of us all. I guess if she's here, it's because this is where the fight is. She is the Knight Errant and her Holy Grail is Justice. She serves no particular King. She has knelt to no man or god. She believes only in the Power of Love. Or, at least, she used to believe in Love.

I have repeatedly told Chloe that I am not Lilith, but to no avail. She admitted to me that her Fairy Godmother had said something about

Lilith being 'herd consciousness' or 'species consciousness' but that was too complicated for Chloe, so she decided I was Lilith because I was an outlaw and I kicked ass. She's made up her mind, and, once her mind is made up, there is no point in trying to talk sense.

I've decided that Lily has come to our little cabin to pass judgment upon us all. She is going through some kind of transformation. She is changing from Cyndi Lauper to Alanis Morrissette; which is to say, she's going from the girl who 'just wants to have fun' to the 'girl who plays GOD'.[6] She has stopped eating and given up bathing. She sits in the Lotus position all day seeking her 'center'. The events in Room 244 hit her harder than she will admit. She genuinely believes there is a fight between Good and Evil coming, and she must defend the Good. She becomes more distant, and frankly, unbearable with each passing day.

I got in the habit of rising early each day to deal with my morning ablutions down at Chloe's Creek, as we had come to call it. Herds of deer would gather at dawn to drink. I would often share words of wisdom with them as I bathed in the middle of the pond. Even in the deepest parts of the pond, the water only came up to the nipples of my perky little breasts. Although I spoke softly, my words carried around the pond to my captive audience.

"What did Thomas Grey mean by, 'Ignorance is bliss'? You may well ask. Thank you for the question.

As we gather here on this quiet, lovely morning, you are blissfully unaware that there are hunters finishing up their breakfasts and getting into trucks to come HERE for the express purpose of KILLING DEER!"

A few skittish colts bolted, but we all know a placid herd seldom heeds a prophet.

"Don't feel bad, my antlered friends. There are hunters out there who are sharpening their knives and preparing to hunt ME today, as well. The only difference is that I am aware of them and I'm anxious as hell.

The question is: which of us is better off? Does my self-awareness give me the advantage of running away before they get here? The fact

---

6 Alanis Morrissette played GOD in the movie *Dogma*.

is, I'm as fenced in as you are. To hide, I would have to deny who I am. I would have to deny the women of the world the immense pleasure of the Legendary Lothario. I could never commit such a crime against humanity."

"Are you diddling yourself right now?" Starr yelled at me from the shore. "You should be 'cause you sure are in love with yourself."

The deer disappeared.

"Come on in and find out," I called back. I started walking towards her. I was doing my best <u>Phoebe Cates coming out of the pool</u> from *Fast times at Ridgemont High.* I pulled my hair back as water streamed off of me. I had recently celebrated my thirtieth birthday, but if she squinted just right…

I walked out of the water and stood before her like Venus on the half-shell. The last time I had stood before her naked like this, I had been sixteen and madly in love with her. I was no longer an innocent young flower waiting to be plucked. I was older, more experienced, but just as ready. Then Starr turned on the buzz-kill.

"I hear your little friend, Dawn, is getting married…to a man."

Obviously, Starr still cared enough to twist the knife in me every chance she got.

I ask you again, deer audience, "Is Ignorance Bliss?"

"Lucky said a funny thing a while ago," she continued, oblivious to my discomfort. "She said you still loved me."

I was astounded and flabbergasted. And not just at her statement. As she spoke, a tall man with a blond crew-cut threw a bag over her head. Before I could blink, Starr had elbowed him, karate-chopped his carotid artery, and kicked him in the solar plexus. He hit the ground like a bag of concrete.

I was grabbed around the neck and felt hard metal at my temple.

"I'm afraid I need you to stop killing that idiot and carry him to that van for me," Donna Dinkwater said from behind me. "If you don't, I'm afraid I'll have to… well, you get the picture."

Starr looked at me and, almost imperceptibly, lifted her right shoulder. I knew what she was telling me. Starr was telling me to use the old "grab the gun and throw your assailant over your shoulder" maneuver. I also knew that the maneuver was only successful about 50% of the time. I couldn't remember what percentage ended up with the captive getting her brains blown out, and I wasn't going to find out.

Starr shrugged and picked up the limp body of Andy Karp and threw it over her shoulder. I was shoved and march-stepped behind Starr to the white panel truck, which sat nearby, with its back doors open.

"Be careful of his…" Donna said, then shuddered when his head hit the back of the van as Starr threw him in.

"Now get in behind him."

Starr stepped all over Andy Karp as she entered the van. I don't know if the kick she gave his head was intentional or accidental.

"Now you," Donna said as she pushed me into the van. I sat next to Starr on a bench on the side of the van.

"She's five- two and weighs less than a hundred pounds," Starr said, disgustedly, "You shoulda took her."

"I'm 5'4"," Donna said, and slammed the back of the van. She got into the passenger seat next to the driver, Stan March. "GO," she said.

When we had been driving for a couple of minutes, I asked, "Where are we going?"

The driver laughed. "Like I would tell you," he scoffed.

I looked at Starr and smiled.

"They didn't even reconnoiter the scene," she said, with that beautiful, delightful smile I fell in love with fourteen years ago.

"We didn't have time," Donna said, beginning to look worried. We drove straight down from the 19th Hole to your cabin and saw you and this one by the pond. John said to grab you and drive south away from the 19th Hole. What's going on here?"

They were as blissful in their ignorance as the deer had been earlier, lapping up their water. I decided to destroy that bliss.

"This road was made for one purpose only; to check the fences around the perimeter of the deer park. It's basically a one-way circle. In an hour, you'll be driving by the hut where you picked us up on your way back to the 19th Hole and the State Police. There is only one entrance and one exit to White Tail Ranch and the 19th Hole is it!"

Donna began yelling into her walkie-talkie. "John, we have a problem!"

"I heard. I heard. Listen, in about ten minutes, you'll see a place where the trees have been cleared for power lines. The towers are huge. The swath of cleared land is at least fifty feet. We'll have to go cross-country."

There was no road to the cleared area of land. When we got stuck in a ditch, Donna made us get out and push the van out of the rut. Finally, we were on the cleared area of land.

"I wish I had a Jeep," Stan March grumbled.

"Yeah," I replied, "It'll be Jeeps coming after us."

"SHUT UP!" Donna and Starr shouted together. Donna was probably just scared, but I guess Starr didn't want them knowing that, by now, a dozen U.N. troops, conscripted by my dad, had been dispatched in six jeeps to rescue us. Anne was in constant touch with us in the cabin, and dad's troops had been on alert for days. They would have split at my cabin and whichever way we went, three would be following us and three would be cutting us off. If John Dinkwater hadn't discovered the power lines, the kidnappers would have been trapped.

Of course, he never would have discovered the power line escape route if I hadn't alerted them to the danger they were in. Me and my big mouth.

Of course, there's information and there's disinformation: "The helicopter 'fly over' from the boys at Red River Army Depot should be here any second," I lied. Starr raised her eyebrows, but Donna bought it.

"Pull over, Stan. I'm going to take the hostages on foot from here on. You and Andy try to find a way out. If they stop you, tell them you just made a wrong turn. Try to convince them you don't know anything."

"Do what?"

We got out and Stan March went lurching off in the van.

Lily was not the pretty Polynesian cheerleader she had been six months before. She covered herself from head to toe with a voluminous black dress that had belonged to the gamekeeper's wife thirty years ago. She had deep thoughts and asked, "What is Truth?" half a dozen times a day.

She began to take long walks alone. (Which was alright by the rest of us.) She would go further every day. One day she discovered Connie chasing a squirrel.

"How many lifetimes have you lived?" she asked.

"As a human? I can't remember. Maybe forty or fifty."

"Now, let me get this straight (and please don't think I'm criticizing). You've lived all those lives and you are barely human. Doesn't that prove that reincarnation is a waste of time?

"How many lifetimes will it take for you to understand that things are not what they seem," Connie replied. "You insist on seeing what's happening here as the Savior of the World talking to a dog-lady. Get over yourself! Try to see one of your many teachers trying to show you the way.

As far as reincarnation being a waste of time, how can you waste something you have an infinite supply of?

Lily decided to move in with Connie and Misty.

Philippa was in a bad mood. "Get rid of your male," she told Bonnie. "Agatha and Mildred are coming and they're allergic to pets." Philippa had wanted her sisters to come to the Dude Ranch, but they were angry about it, which ruined the whole thing.

Bonnie untied Chris and followed him to the door. She took out her knife and held it to his back. "Don't try anything funny," she warned, and they walked out into the Texas heat.

When they were a block away, Chris said, "Don't try anything funny? Is that the best you could come up with?"

"Up yours, wise-ass."

"So, what do we do now?"

"I have to find a good place to bury you."

"Can we eat first?"

Like all restaurants in all tourist attractions, the front was full of brochures for other tourist attractions. Bonnie took one for <u>White-Tail Ranch</u>.

As they ate, Bonnie read the brochure. "Not for kids," she read, "Guess you can't go." Chris gave her the finger, which kind of proved her point.

"This place is right next to the Dude Ranch. It's huge. Three hundred acres. Plenty of places to bury a body," she said with a wink.

"I've seen that road," Chris said, pointing. "You can see it from the entrance to the Amusement Park. According to the map, that road leads to the 19th Hole."

"That's perfect, Bonnie said, "You could meet your parents there and they could drive you home. I'll tell Phillipa I buried you out on the deer run."

"And what are you going to do, Bonnie?"

"I've got to go back to the old witch."

"You can't be serious."

"She trusts me and I'm the only one who can stop her."

"Stop her from what?"

"She promised Celeste Worthinghampton that she would kill Chloe, and she means to kill Lily as well. I'm going to kill her before she can do either."

"I can't believe you're younger than I am," Chris told her. "You are the bravest girl I've ever known. You're an honest-to-god hero!"

Together, they made their way to the western perimeter of Dickerson's Dude Ranch. Open gates welcomed them to the Wild West Amusement Park. The Amusement Park was open only to foot traffic from the Dude Ranch.

"That's strange," Chris said, "Do you hear a speeding vehicle?"

The road that circled White-Tail Ranch was higher than the ground cut out for the power lines. Stan March was going full speed when he hit the uneven ground. It sent the van airborne. It flew over the road and landed in the entrance to the Amusement Park. He slammed the van right into a statue of Aphrodite outside the Tunnel of Love. He missed Bonnie and Chris by a matter of a few feet.

Stan got out of the van holding a gun. How it ended up in his hands, he had no idea. Stan was a wheelman. He'd never shot a gun in his life.

Nevertheless, it was a brave thing that Bonnie did when she ran into him, tackled him to the ground, and took the gun away from him.

"I'm a real fucking hero," she thought to herself.

The crowd surrounded her applauding. They lifted her up and carried her off, chanting, "Our Hero! Our Hero!"

Betty Lou Holcum handcuffed the perps and checked the gun. It was empty.

CHAPTER TWENTY-ONE

THE ENEMY OF MY ENEMY'S ENEMY

The Portland Coven of the Dianic Wiccan Church moved quietly, in single file, across the golf course. There was no one around at midnight to see them, but their leader, Judith, insisted that they keep their masks handy. She wore hers all the time. The women (for there were no male members of this militaristic, anti-male, coven) wore long black gowns and Guy Fawkes masks when they were on a mission.

This was a protection mission. Each member of the team carried two pictures in their pockets at all times. One of them was a picture of Lily Inouye in her TCU cheerleading uniform. Judith had made each member swear to her personally to protect this girl with their life. The other picture was of Chloe Dunnally/Williams.

"The Church has requested that we protect this individual, as well," Judith told them.

There was no hesitation as they neared the moat that had been built to keep the deer off the golf course. Judith knew, from careful reconnaissance, that the moat was no more than four or five feet deep at any point. Past the moat was the road that ran from the 19th Hole to the deer park, itself. One at a time, they ran across the road and into the trees beyond. From there, they kept the 10 ft. fence to their right and made their way to the pond on the western end of the ranch. They set up camp on the north side of the pond.

"Make yourselves comfortable," Judith told them, "but no fires. Keep your eyes on the small building on the east side of the pond. Keep track of who goes in and who goes out. Maintain the location of Lily, um, and the other one, at all times. If my intelligence is correct, we may have to defend that shack from a small army.

"Small army" might have been a slight exaggeration. Chuck "Bent Nose" Benson (always the coward) had hired four hoods who would kill a baby for a cigarette butt. They had signed up for a weekend of Deer Hunting. They wore bright orange vests and carried high-powered weapons. Chuck's plan was to walk up to the hut and start shooting until everyone inside was dead. Subtlety was not Chuck's strong suit. All he had to do then was kill the remaining members of the Dinkwater Gang and collect the $300,000 from Stanley Scovall. ("Bent Nose" was as yet unaware of Mr. Scovall's demise.)

Dawn's phone rang at ten o'clock at night. She was already in bed. George Colter was on a twenty-four shift at the fire station. She assumed it was him, calling to check on her. She almost didn't answer. Then, because there was LITERALLY NOTHING ELSE to do, she picked up.

"Dawn?" a tremulous, childlike voice asked, "is it because the chicken thinks life will be better across the road?"

"MISTY! How did you get my number? Never mind, what's wrong? Are you OK?"

"Hi, Dawn. I'm OK but Lily needs you."

"Lily needs me? The last time she saw me, she practically spit on me. She cast me out like a worn-out dildo."

"Do those things get some wear and tear on them? Maybe Nadia and I should start shopping around..."

"What's wrong with Lily."

"She's let herself go something awful. She doesn't eat, she doesn't sleep, she doesn't bathe. She just sits in a lotus position and mumbles. Every once in a while, I see a tear roll down her cheek. I think she's scared, Dawn. I think she needs someone who can give her confidence for the battle to come."

"What battle?"

"Oh, it's coming. I live in a cave a mile away and I can feel it. There is definitely a battle coming."

Donna is definitely straight. We've been wandering around the wilds of "White-Tail Ranch" for nearly 48 hours, and she hasn't succumbed to my blandishments, so she's either straight or has some kind of Superhuman strength.

I have got her to open up a little, though. Her and, especially, her brother John, see petty crime as the family business. Their father was a famous cat burglar. He once stole a pink diamond that was quite valuable. The problem was her brother was just not particularly good at it.

"We should have had Starr in Fort Worth by now, holding her for ransom," Donna admitted.

"And me, right? Starr and me."

"Well, frankly ma'am, John kinda promised that you would be killed in the kidnapping attempt. He never meant to do it, though! We don't even carry loaded weapons."

"You…that gun's not loaded?"

"No ma'am."

"Then why in the hell am I walking around with my hands up?"

"I don't know, ma'am."

"Look, Donna, why don't you just give it up. Your accomplices in the van are probably incarcerated by now, your brother is probably dying from heatstroke and dehydration; Hell, WE would be if Starr hadn't shown us how to track deer to find water… What's so funny?"

"For your information, Miss Know-it-all, my brother is under covers in the 19th Hole, pumping the proprietress for information."

"Her name wouldn't happen to be Anne, would it?"

"I don't know. My phone has lost its charge, but the last time I talked to him, he said she was a beautiful, sexy woman who thought he looked a lot like George Clooney."

"Yeah, that's Anne. I'm sure he's pumping her, but I'll bet he's not getting any useful information. Donna, listen. It's true that Virgil would love to see me dead. But what he really wants is for you to keep Starr from that cabin."

"What cabin?"

"That one across the pond. There."

"Damn. We're back where we started. This is the pond where we grabbed you."

"I'm going," Starr said, speaking for the first time since we arrived at the pond. "There's a toothbrush with my name on it in there."

"It actually says 'Princess Leia'," I told Donna, in case she took Starr literally.

Donna was a good sport about it, and the three of us entered the cabin.

Chloe was sitting at the table, writing something. She was wearing one of my favorite summer dresses. It was white with little black peace signs and yellow smiley faces all over it. Lucky was on the phone.

"She's right here," she said and handed me the phone.

"Nice dress," I said to Chloe, as I walked by.

"Nice miasma," she replied, holding her nose.

"Hey, the last time I bathed, I was kidnapped," I told her, "Thanks for looking for me."

"I can't go out. I'm a target." Then she stuck her tongue out at me.

"Hello," I said, taking the phone.

"Hey, If you're through arguing with the child, I got some things to tell ya," Anne said.

"Shoot."

First of all, the Dinkwater Gang is supposed to try to kidnap Starr."

"Old news, girlfriend. They already did. Officially, we are kidnap victims."

"The thing is, they were never meant to succeed. They were just supposed to keep Starr busy while Chuck "Bent Nose" Benton killed you."

"How do you know this?"

"Virgil Wilder is spending a promotional Free Golf Weekend at the 19th Hole. One of my best girls 'fell in love' with him shortly after his arrival. She mixed him up a little cocktail that included Rohypnol and Pentothal. Boy, does that guy hate you!"

"Me? I just teach at-risk kids that they are loved. I know he hates that kind of heresy, but does he hate it badly enough to kill me? Or does it go back to our little tussle in high school?

"I got the impression it's gone beyond 'Obstruction of Justice'. Virgil has heard that there is about to be a lot of blood spilled on that old deer lease and he wants to make sure some of it is yours."

"I seriously regret overreacting to his advances that night," I said, "but it was fourteen years ago, for fucks sake! Can't he just move on?"

"You didn't diddle that red and blue haired girl, did you?"

"Oh, my God. One time. She was just experimenting."

There were some 'popping' sounds from across the pond.

"What the hell's that," Chloe asked and went to the front door. She stepped out on the porch and saw Mannie Pep running towards the shack. He recognized her and drew out a knife.

"You Bitch!" he screamed, "You shot Mo!"

She was going to point out that Mo shot his own self in the foot, but before she could, he grabbed her and raised the knife.

Then the side of his face exploded.

Across the road, Chuck "Bent Nose" Benton said, "Damn! Missed again."

We later learned that "Bent Nose" was shooting at my white dress with the black and yellow designs on it. He had seen me wearing it earlier. He couldn't make out the designs because he was extremely far-sighted.

CHAPTER TWENTY-TWO

DUELING REALITIES

Officer Holcum had the entire front porch area of my humble abode roped off with police tape. Unfortunately, unless we went through a window, the crime scene was our only way in or out. It was bound to be contaminated before the morning was done.

"The shot came from over yonder," Officer Holcum said, indicating a roped-off area across the road. "It was a high-powered rifle, such as is common with hunters around here."

"So, your theory is that Manny was shot accidentally by a near-sighted hunter?" I asked, incredulously.

"No ma'am, I'm afraid it was something a lot more serious than that."

Officer Holcum's little sister came walking across the road.

"There are a bunch of cigarette butts over there," she said, "looks like the perp was waiting for someone to come out of the shack. He recognized your distinctive sun-dress before he had a chance to see her face."

"He thought he had you in his sights," Betty Lou informed me.

"But the young fella jumped in front of her," Officer Holcum said.

"Bet she'll stay out of my stuff, now."

"What were the popping sounds we heard," Lucky asked.

"See that little clearing on the north side of the lake?" Officer Holcum replied. "Six or seven individuals camped out there last night.

When they saw the victim rushing the cabin, they tried to stop him. The problem was they were using little 22 caliber pea-shooters. They didn't have to range. Most of their bullets fell harmlessly into the pond."

"They're long gone now," Betty Lou informed us. "We'll probably never see them again."

Judith's binoculars were set on maximum. From two hundred yards away, she could see the vaccination scar on Lily's arm. From her vantage point atop a 60 ft. electrical tower, Judith could see the small hill where the naiad cave was situated. She saw Connie and Misty rolling down the hill, playing some rough game. Lily just sat by the cave entrance, her arms wrapped around her legs, her chin upon her knees. She was dressed in black and appeared to be sad.

Judith set the binoculars down and wiped her face. Up here, totally alone, she had removed her Guy Fawkes's mask. Even without it, it was hot. Her face was sweating profusely, especially around her fake nose.

A movement at the bottom of the hill caught her attention. She saw a Fort Worth Police car pull up. As she reached for her binoculars, she saw Connie and Misty making a beeline for the cave. They gabbled something at Lily as they ran by. Judith recognized the cop who got out, though she was not in uniform. It was Dawn Hightower, one of the groupies that hung out with the lesbian vigilante gang. The cop walked up to the entrance to the cave and stood in front of Lily.

Judith used her UZI-OD-1 Observation Listening Devise to listen in on their conversation:

"Hi. I'm Dawn. You may not remember me. Perhaps I'd look more familiar like this..." and, with that, the cop prostrated herself before Lily.

Lily laughed. And a cloud moved out of the way of the sun and the entire hillside was covered in light.

Dawn smiled and sat up next to Lily. "So, this horse walks into a bar..." she began.

Lily shook her head. "Did you drive all the way from Fort Worth to ask about my long face?"

"No, I came here because Misty is worried about you."

"Misty. What a beautiful soul! You know, for twenty-two years I thought I was the most miserable person in the world. My dad beat my mom regularly and, if I tried to help her, he beat me too. I was afraid to tell them I was in love with a girl named Scout. All the while, I lived in middle-class suburbia, had an allowance, went to good schools. I thought it was awful.

Meanwhile, Misty was stealing lunch money because her mom was too wacked-out on drugs to feed her. She had to lock her bedroom door when her mother had a date. Sometimes, she had to escape out her window and spend the night in the streets. Yet, she always has a smile on her face!

Do you know that she and her wet-nosed friend have more fun in an hour than I had in twenty-two years? The best time in my life were the few weeks I spent with her band. And now..."

"Now you have a superpower," Nan finished.

"Ha. Yeah, well, if you call insanity a superpower, I guess I do."

"So, you remember what you saw in the motel room."

"I'll never forget it. It was like something from a horror show. I had never seen anything so frightening."

"Did you see yourself?"

"What do you mean?"

"You transformed as well. Chloe saw it. She told me. What she described was exactly the vision I saw with the blue-haired Irish girl when we dropped acid."

"Oh, well. That explains it."

"OK. I admit that the drugs made me misinterpret the vision. I turned it into some kind of religious Vision Quest. But you are unmistakably from beyond this bland, gray existence we call Reality. And, you have the ability to see the moral essence of creatures' souls."

————— ❖ —————

Chloe went around to everyone in the cabin. "You're an elder," she said, "You're an elder. You're an elder." Then she called for a meeting of the Elders.

"I'm not even a member of your church," Donna objected.

"You can't talk," Chloe told her, "The Chair does not recognize you."

"I'm Donna Dinkwater…" Chloe held her hands over her ears and went, "Na-na-na, can't hear you."

Lucky looked at me and said, "Move to strike."

"Motion seconded."

Lucky pretended to swipe at Chloe, but Starr stood and got between them.

"You're out of order."

"I was working fine this morning."

"Has anyone seen Lily," I asked.

"We don't need her," Chloe said. "We have a quorum."

"Isn't there a motion on the table?" Donna asked.

"Don't you mean 'on the floor'?" Starr wanted to know.

"There's a motion on the floor to table this meeting," I announced. "GODDAMN IT. EVERYBODY SHUT UP!"

Chloe really knows how to work a room. Everybody shut up and listened to the red-faced kid.

"Thank you. Thank you. As you are all aware, today, for the first time in the History of the Church, blood has been spilled."

"It was just Mannie Pep," Starr mentioned.

"What did you do with the dress that got all the blood on it?" I asked Chloe.

"It's in the trash. You'll never get those bloodstains out. What would you do with it?"

"I'm going to tie it to a stick and use it as a banner when we march off to war."

"That gets me back to the purpose of this meeting. Thanks, Alys."

"It's time for this church to have a 'Mission Statement'."

"I don't think churches have mission statements," Starr said.

"I think they have 'Creeds' or some shit," I said.

"THIS CHURCH IS GOING TO HAVE A GODDAMN MISSION STATEMENT, SO SHUT UP AND LISTEN."

That Chloe has a real way with words. Very eloquent.

"I suggest this," Chloe began when she was sure she had our attention. "Our mission is to provide a worship alternative to the Dogmatic, Paternalistic, and Chauvinistic Christian Church."

"But who is your Savior?" Donna asked.

"We don't need no stinking sacrificial savior," Chloe insisted. "Our church is not a place to try and appease an angry god, but to celebrate a benevolent one, who brings us True Equality.

Chloe and I kinda invented this religion between us, so I felt no compunction about helping out with the rules.

"The #1 rule is obvi: **No Men Allowed**," I announced.

"Sounds like my eight-year-old niece's tea club." Donna snorted.

I looked around the table to see how we were going to handle this heretic. What I saw were three faces displaying complete agreement."

"Think about it, Alys. You can't discriminate. It's just wrong."

"That's it," Chloe decreed, "Men are in."

"And I'm out," I stated and walked out the door.

I started to step off the porch, but there was nothing there. A sheer cliff fell into a bottomless abyss. About thirty or forty yards away, two old crones flew at me on brooms. I ran to the side of the porch and jumped over the rail…into a pit of writhing snakes. I climbed out of the pit with snakes crawling in and out of my clothes. Panic rose. They were trying to GET INSIDE ME!

I knew I was losing my mind, but I told myself I was going to take at least one old hag with me. I struggled to get back on the porch, but hundreds of rats were jumping off, jumping on to me, on to my face, wiggling under my arms. I wanted to scream but feared they would run into mouth.

"You must fight them," I heard Lilith tell me. *"Open your eyes and **LOOK** at them. DO IT, ALYS! I'm giving you my power. Now **FIGHT!**'*

I opened my eyes. I forced myself to ignore the creepy-crawly things on me. I focused on the yard I knew must be there in front of me. I took a step into nothing…and my foot touched solid ground. Now, I saw the front yard. Now, I saw the little, white, picket fence that surrounded it. As reality returned, the witches began to look like two old hags. They advanced towards me, but I could tell they were losing confidence.

Armed with the laws of science and a healthy skepticism, I stood in the middle of the yard and awaited them.

"Go back to your Sam's Club wine and your After-School TV movies, old ladies.

I hit them with the Pythagorean Theorem and Schrodinger's Cat. Agatha stumbled to her knees, and I blasted Mildred with the Second Law of Thermodynamics. Blood ran out of her ears.

"I think. Therefore, I AM," I screamed, triumphantly; and Mildred's head exploded.

I walked up to the kneeling Agatha. "Do unto others as you would have them do unto you."

She shuddered one last foul breath and died.

I looked down the road and saw Lily standing there. She looked exhausted.

I convinced Lily to sleep in the cabin that night. I promised her I would check on Connie and Misty. I filled an ice chest with Coors Light and took the jeep to their cave. They were eating a rabbit that Connie had caught. When they saw me, Connie whispered, "Witchslayer" and Misty knelt on one knee. It was kind of cool. Then, Connie pushed Misty over and they started rough-housing and the spell was broken. Still, it felt good to be a hero.

I carried the ice chest to the top of the hill and sat under a tree and did some thinking. I'm not one given to introspection, but I felt the need right then to examine the basic precept of my life: which is that my dad is the greatest guy in the world and has loved me every second of my life.

When dad was in prison, there was a lot of talk among strangers about what a crook he was. When he was released, there was some talk among my so-called friends that he might not be as good a man as I thought. When Stanley Scovall tried to kidnap Irene Worthinghampton, Dad put all that talk to rest.

It was revealed at that time that dad was a Commander in the United Nation's Armed Forces and had been working undercover for years to break up an international currency counterfeiting ring. Dad broke up the kidnapping attempt, as well. Mr. Worthinghampton declared him a hero. Everybody took back all the mean things they had been saying about dad.

(Dad was actually really lucky that the kidnappers were the notoriously inept Dinkwater Gang. They had intended to kidnap me but fucked up and kidnapped Aggie Goodman by mistake. When no one showed any interest in paying a ransom for Aggie, they released her with red faces.)

Dad was finally recognized by the world as the great man he was… until the day I left a meeting with Mr. W and tried to find Anne for a quicky.

I crushed a beer can and threw it at the ice chest. It missed. I went over to the ice chest and bent over to retrieve another beer. I missed. I feel to the ground. The dizzy, sick, feeling that came over me reminded me of the way I felt when I walked out of Mr. W's suite and saw my dad schmoozing with Anne Baldwin. I jumped back into the suite. Mr. W's receptionist looked at me. "Bill-collectors," I explained. She went back to work.

I called dad. "Hi, dad, how're you doing?"

"Actually, I'm really busy. You know we showed our hand too soon with the kidnap thing. I'm not authorized to use UN troops on American soil. I gotta get those guys outta there toots sweet (sic). Don't worry, I'll be there myself to protect you as soon as I get this mess straightened out.

"So, you're close by?"

"Yeah, baby. I'm in Room 214 of the 19th Hole.

The floor level of the 19th Hole is just one, big casino. The first floor of rooms is actually the second floor, and the rooms open up to a big veranda where you can look down on the action when you leave your room. I found a place at the slots where I had a good view of Room #214. It was a heart-crusher, but not that big of a surprise, when an hour later, I saw Anne walk out.

—————⟡—————

"Are you crying?"

I looked up and Misty was standing there.

"No, sweetie, I'm, um, just looking for a stick. Can you help me?"

"How about this one?"

"No, not big enou…here! This is perfect." I took the big old stick in my hand. This was the kind of bat Babe Ruth hit homers with. I took it in a two-hand grip and gave it a few practice swings.

Then, I MURDERED that fucking ice chest! I stove in the top and smashed the sides. Whenever a beer would roll out, I would attack it and beat it to death. Finally, I tossed the stick as far down the hill as I could. It stopped a disappointing ten feet away. I wished I could try another throw. Then, the sickening, dark, heavy realization smothered me like a CIA agent waterboarding a terrorist, THERE ARE NO DO-OVERS! You can't go back and change one little jot or tittle (or is it 'tiddle'?)

"Is there anything wrong, ma'am?"

"Just one little thing, hon. You see, daddies are supposed to bring their little princess ponies for her birthday. They are supposed to make sure she has beautiful clothes and nice friends. They are supposed to give them Ivy League educations and handsome husbands. They are _not_ SUPPOSED TO HAVE THE SAME TASTE IN SEXUAL PARTNERS THAT SHE DOES!"

CHAPTER TWENTY-THREE

The Dinkwater Gang Strikes Again

Donna was bathing in the pond at sunset. She hated nature but was standing in water that had things swimming around in it. The mud squishing around her toes was disgusting, but it was better than trying to get a shower in the cabin. There were three lesbians there. (Not that there was anything wrong with that, she said to herself, thinking of Jerry Seinfeld and George Costanza.) She didn't have to worry about them here. She just had to worry about things like snakes.

Which is why she nearly jumped out of her skin when she heard a hiss from the nearby bushes.

"Psst. Just act normal, somebody might be watching."

"DON'T hiss at me like a snake, John! I swear you made me pee a bit."

"Just keep acting like you're bathing and listen: The cops got Andy and Stan. This caper is blown. We need to get out of here."

"What about the $300,000?"

"Hey, it didn't work out this time. What can you do?"

"Dad would be so disappointed in you, John."

"Don't start, Donna. I'm sick of hearing what a failure I am. I'm also sick and tired of hearing what you could have done if you were the older brother. Just spare me."

"Go ahead. Quit. I'll take that $300,000 and enroll at the Police Academy."

John blanched. "You wouldn't! Dad would turn over in his grave."

"Dad was cremated."

"Listen, Dawn. This thing is bigger than we imagined. Factions are deciding who will be in charge of the newest force in religious thinking, since Martin Luther King nailed his 'Ninety-five Theses' to the door of Saint Paul's Basilica…"

"First of all, John, that never happened, and, secondly, this isn't even about all that."

"Um, I beg to differ with you, sis. I had an opportunity to talk to Commander Loxley and he tells me that some powerful movers and shakers are behind what's going on here. These next few days could be the most decisive since the Cuban Missile Crisis."

"Wow. Aren't you Mr. Hyperbole, today? You just don't get it. What's going on is much more important than politics or religion. You males can't see the forest for the Playboy centerfolds."

"And what, pray tell, is more important than the possibility of a militant feminist group taking over the most influential new religion since…"

"Oh God, tell me he's not going to go there."

"…Christianity."

(He did it.) "John, don't you wonder what made Cathy Anderson lose her grip on reality and slide back into the persona of 'Catherine of Aragon'?

"Cathy Anderson? Well, I thought she was really close with the lately departed Mr. Scoville (sic)."

"Yes. But was that it or was it that she saw the love triangle becoming more isosceles and not so much equilateral."

"I have no idea what the fuck you're talking about, Donna."

"I'm talking about the Alys/Starr/Cathy axis, of course. Could you not see things heating up between Starr and Alys, lately?"

"WHAT? I've been up to my neck in lawmen, hunters, vigilante lesbians, and East Texas chiggers! I haven't had time for Soap Operas."

"So, I suppose you are not even aware that Dawn has possessed Nan's body?"

"This is common knowledge?"

"Alys's torch for Starr is Olympic-sized. It hasn't been extinguished in twenty years. You look at Starr and you wonder, 'Is she starting to realize that Alys can't help being Alys? Is she considering forgiving her and accepting her as she is?' I'm telling you, John, it's an exciting time to be alive!"

"Jesus, Donna. You are such a *girl*."

"W.A.W.W.A. W. Which witch would you want?"

"I must speak to Agatha or Mildred Borgia."

"Um, I'm afraid they are unavailable at the moment. Is there some way I can help you?"

"Please inform the Borgia sisters that the Portland Coven has been hijacked! I am Hester Prim, the High Priestess of the Portland Coven. I was beaten and left for dead just outside a godforsaken little tourist trap called Dickinson's Dude Ranch, in East Texas. I just woke up in the hospital this morning and the coven is gone. Philippa personally asked me to protect Lilith…"

"Excuse me, are you in contact with Philippa Borgia?"

"No, I…"

"The truth is Miss, Agatha and Mildred have dropped off the radar and Phillipa is what we like to call a 'witch of interest' in the case. If you have any information about the whereabouts of Phillipa Borgia, Celeste Worthinghampton would very much like to hear from you. Hello?"

John told Donna that he had hidden their car in bushes by the side of the road about a mile up the road towards the 19th Hole. They both had keys. He told her to use the car to escape if the heat got too bad.

"I'm going to hang out with the Commander for a while. They've pulled out his troops and left him alone to protect his daughter. We know that Virgil Wilder has hired some thugs to kill her. Back in Fort Worth, Virgil pretends to be a 'Law and Order' District Attorney, but Commander Loxley says that Virgil's hatred is more personal. Anyway, the car's there if you need it."

Dawn decided to check it out. She wanted to make sure she could find it in a hurry, and she wanted to make sure it would start, had gas, etc. She came around a bend in the road and saw a bizarre sight.

Six or seven kids in long, black robes with Guy Fawkes masks were swarming Starr like bees on honey. One of them held a rag over her nose and she went limp. Then the anarchist insects produced a stretcher and carried her off into the woods. Donna jumped about a foot when a voice behind her said:

"Can you believe that shit?"

"Who the fuck are you," Donna gasped.

"Hi, I'm Bonnie. You haven't seen a big, white guy out here, have you? His name's Chris."

Donna's mind would not process that information. "Never mind big white guys named Chris: that was Starr. She's supposed to be in my custody. What's the deal with the kids in the Halloween masks? Are they a cult? Do they know about the..."

"Do they know about what?"

"Never mind. Bonnie? What are you doing out here in the middle of nowhere?"

"I'm a hero. I'm going to save Alys from the homophobic D.A."

"You want to help me save Starr?"

"Sure. Let's do it."

On the very southernmost tip of Whitetail Ranch, there is a barn. In the late summer it is filled with bales of hay. The hay is distributed by cowboys (deerboys?) during the winter months to keep the deer alive when there is nothing else to eat. The barn is also where Commander

Loxley decided to bivouac during his stay. It is also where he kept various military items, he had expropriated from the United Nations Peace-Keeping Force of North America.

Chris Hanlon was checking out a cool fifty caliber machine gun mounted on the back of a jeep, when Commander Loxley drove up in his Cadillac Escalade. When the Commander opened the door, Chris caught sight of the beautiful Anne Baldwin, whom he'd met at the 19th Hole.

"Hi, Chris," she called.

"Help me carry this stuff in," the Commander said to Chris and said, "I'll be right back," to Anne.

They carried a bunch of monitors and screens into the barn. As the Commander worked setting things up, he said to Chris,

"I've hunted lions in Africa, elephants in India, wildebeests in Asia; but you know what the hardest prey to trap is?" Evidently, it was a rhetorical question because he answered himself- "Man. You know why?"

"Because of your common humanity and brotherhood?"

"Hell, no. It's because to capture a creature, you must be able to think like that creature. It's difficult for me to think like a weaselly creep like the 'Bent Nose' fella, but I think a cowardly henchman would probably position 4 or 5 rapscallions here (and he pointed at the monitor he had just activated) with heavy automatic weapons, and simply, open fire when she walks out the front door.

"She's always in that hut," Alys's dad continued, "She's working on her new novel right now. I tried to pitch an idea for a story about Henry VI, you know, the 'Mad King'? She shot it down, though. She says she doesn't want to write about someone who "lost his wits, his two kingdoms, and his only son". She's beginning work on a novel about Eleanor Roosevelt and her dear friend, Lorena Hickok. (I saw a couple of pages that described a fantastical dream sequence involving a threesome with Amelia Earhart.)

She walks around the pond in the evening and bathes in it in the mornings, but other than that, she's always in the hut. I'll personally be there to protect her at those times, but the rest of time it's simply a matter of watching this monitor and these others of the surrounding terrain.

Listen, old chap, my lady and I have an appointment we simply can't get out of. Would you be so good as to keep an eye on this monitor and alert me if anything happens? You've got my number, right? Splendid. Listen, I've installed some booby-traps in the area, so don't go out there yourself. If you can't reach me, here's the key to the jeep."

"The one with the 50-caliber mounted on the back?"

"That's the one."

"You got it, sir."

Chloe hung up the phone with a heavy heart. If the information had not come from Martha Mendosa, she would not have believed it.

Martha had received a phone call from a Captain O'Brien of the FBI. In a French accent that sounded like it had been stolen from Steve Martin, he had informed her that the FBI had long had the two missing witches, Agatha, and Mildred Borgia, under surveillance. They had recorded every phone call, both incoming and outgoing. In light of recent activity, Captain O'Brien thought he should share the information with Starr, for her outstanding service to the FBI. He revealed the substance of a thirty second phone call made from DFW airport just a few days after the death of Stanley Scovall.

Chloe listened to the taped conversation for the 10th time. There could be no doubt in her mind: the voice revealing Lily's hidden location was that of her beloved au pair, Scout.

O'Brien had provided the address and phone number of the exclusive sanitarium where Cathy was being treated. Scout was still with her.

Chloe sat down and wrote her this missive:

Dear Scout,

Unlike the original Quasimodo, you were once beautiful
and kind. Whenever my stepmother was mean to me,
you always comforted me. How that sweet girl would
loath the adult version of herself. Your twisted jealousy

has put many people in danger, including me. When I was seven, you held my hand and promised me you would never let anyone hurt me. Now, your great capacity for love has been perverted to hatred because your erstwhile Esmeralda has found happiness with others. How can you live with yourself when you, like Iago, are "devoid of conscience, with no remorse"? May you live a million lifetimes as a cockroach.

Your Former Admirer, Chloe

Donna and Bonnie followed the Portland gang to their hide-out. Starr's captors were kind to her, but leery. They released from the stretcher and gave her water. Eventually, they led her to the main tent, where their leader waited. Seconds later there was a scream. Donna and Bonnie looked at each other with consternation.

The consternation turned to panic when the cries within the tent became the sounds of combat, and the sides of the tent would pooch out on one side and then the other as bodies bounced off them. They rushed from their hidings place and ran to the tent, but the robed figures prevented them from interfering.

"Hester wanted to deal with the infidel herself," they were told.

The tent ripped open in the front and two struggling women came falling out.

"Her name's not fucking HESTOR," Starr cried. "Does this look like your fucking leader?" she asked, as she ripped the mask off the other one.

The once pretty face of Julie Frazier was made grotesque by the prosthetic nose that was dangling by a thread.

"This is your doing!" Julie screamed at Starr. "You shot my nose off and then you killed Stanley. I'll have my revenge," she swore, and then, she ran, laughing maniacally, into the dense forest of pine trees.

"You were trying to kill him, yourself," Starr called after her, but she had disappeared from sight.

Bonnie thought Chris might be at Alys's cabin, so she took off the next day. Starr, Donna, and the Portland Coven tracked Julie for the next two days. On the third day they got close enough to Commander Loxley's barn to get wi-fi. They got a message from Bonnie:
"Get back here ASAP! Lily is in danger! Hurry!"

CHAPTER TWENTY-FOUR

THE BATTLE OF DEER RUN

I t is no surprise that the first blood spilled that day was mine. Chloe came out on the porch full of good cheer and bonhomie. I contend that her bright "GOOD MORNING" was unnecessarily loud. Perhaps she disagrees. The upshot was, I fell off the porch swing and scraped my elbow rather severely.

We went down to the pond to clean the wound.

"Starr returned last night," Chloe mentioned conversationally. "Oh look, there she is now."

I looked up from the wound on my elbow and saw the tall figure opening the screen door. What happened next appeared in black and white flashes, like photos in an old Police Gazette:

The frazzle-haired, black-clad girl in her red keds, stepping off the porch while adjusting her sunglasses.

A raging Julie Frazier rushing up to her and shooting her, point blank, in the chest.

Bonnie rushing out and heroically grabbing Julie just a second too late.

The hail of bullets from across the street that cut them both down.

It happened in agonizing slow-motion but was over in a second.

Chloe pointed across the road at a man who seemed to fly out of a tree and land on his face. Another, with a rope around his ankle, arced through the air and smashed into a tree. There was an explosion, and another man went flying. Part of him landed in the road.

Suddenly, a jeep appeared coming up the road from the south. Chris Hanlon drove until he was directly in front of the little cottage. He stopped the jeep in the middle of the road and grabbed the 50-caliber mounted on the back.

The cannon-like weapon wouldn't fire. Chris came under heavy fire and was hit.

"Chris!" Chloe gasped. She was up and running before I could react.

"No," I screamed, as she ran towards Chris and certain death.

Lucky later swore that one moment Lily was sitting in the Lotus position in the house and the next instant she was standing in the yard. I saw her there, too, although I could not believe what I saw. She looked to be nine-feet tall. She was naked. There was a huge serpent coiled around her body. Bullets bounced harmlessly off the serpent. She raised her hands and spoke:

"I am Lilith. I am over five thousand years old, and I remember every moment of my existence. My blood is the blood of Adam. It runs through these children here and I tell you they will not die today.

The shooting stopped. Chloe and I dragged Chris into the shack, which had been shot up pretty badly. Blood ran down Lucky's arm, but she said she was OK. I looked outside.

The firing from across the road had stopped. Lily had returned to her old self, wearing the gamekeeper's wife's old dress. She looked like an old, exhausted woman. Nevertheless, she turned to wave at us.

A huge hole appeared in her torso, and almost simultaniously, there was a loud pop in the distance. The barrage of gunfire from across the street began again. The high-caliber munitions were shredding the little shack. Bullets tore through the wall like they were paper. Lucky tried to cover Chris and Chloe with her body but she wasn't going to stop the bullets any more than the walls.

I decided, "Fuck it," and walked out the front door. I couldn't bear to look at the riddled bodies on the porch, but I felt like we owed it to

Lily not to let her body be desicrated by any more violence. I walked towards her body. A hundred rounds were shot as I dragged her inside and put her on the bed in the back room. Not one round hit me. Make of that what you will.

A louder, more booming sort of gunfire began. I looked outside. Dear old dad had manned the 50-caliber and was blowing the shit out "Bent-Nose" and his minions.

The gunfire ceased. My ears were just adjusting to the quiet. I thought I heard someone whistling, "Ding, Dong, the Witch is Dead." I looked down the road and saw Dawn Hightower walking down the road to us. I couldn't make out what she was carrying until she walked into the yard and threw it on the ground.

It was the head of Phillipa Borgia.

I walked around to the back of the shack and sat in the porch swing where I had begun this day.

"Wow. Busy day," I thought to myself. Then just before I could figure out whether hysteria would lead to tears or laughter, Chloe stuck her head out the back door.

"It's not her," she said.

ADDENDUM

<u>Addendum to the Official Police Report</u>
<u>By Captain Rashoman Ockman</u>
<u>Chief Investigator, Criminal Investigations Division</u>
October 16, 2010

The investigation into the events that took place on September 17, 2000 on the grounds of the <u>White-Tail Deer Reserve</u> was the most thorough and exhaustive I've ever been a part of in my twenty-eight years on the Force. It is complete and covers every aspect of one of the bloodiest battles in the annals of Texas crime.

Every spent shell was tagged and photographed. The position and location of every body was meticulously detailed. Who was killed, and by whom was determined as well as possible by forensic science.

This addendum in no way reflects any criticism of the official report. It merely addresses one mysterious question that the report was unable to answer. Eleven people were known to die in what has now come to be known as the "Battle of Deer Run", but only ten bodies were recovered.

What follows is the testimony of the four survivors who witnessed the shooting of Lily Inouye. (For the purpose of complete disclosure, I have included the testimony of the mad woman, Dawn Hightower.)

<u>Witness #1</u>—Lucky Betts (real name-I checked.) Lucky was in the cabin the whole time.

"I was the only one still awake when Scout arrived. Chloe had gone to bed early because she was so bored, and Alys was already passed out on the back porch. I was really stoked to see her, but Lily was freaked. She really thought, at first, that Scout was there to kill her. She calmed down after a while and the two of them started whispering, so, I volunteered to 'secure the perimeter' like it was something we always did at three am. When I got back inside, they were more relaxed and just sitting there drinking. The story they gave me was that Chloe had called Cathy because she was worried about Lily. She supposedly told Cathy that the only thing keeping Scovall's troops away from Lily and Alys was their fear of Starr. Scout had volunteered to beef up security.

It sounded fishy to me because Scout was not a threat of any kind to anyone. She was as tall as Starr, but she was all girlie-girl and wouldn't do much but swat at the bad guys with her purse. Anyway, we told her about Starr being MIA for a few days and how much safer we would feel when she got back.

I was just joking when I suggested Scout dress up like Starr and pretend to be her in the morning, but Lily and Scout thought it was a great idea.

"If the thugs that Virgil Wilder hired think Starr is here, they won't attack. If we can hold off a few more days, Commander Loxley might be back with more reinforcements," Lily suggested.

"I'm not as dark as my mom was," Scout said, helping herself to more gin. "I often pass for white. If I covered myself with Goth clothing like Starr, I bet those goons wouldn't know the difference."

"We would have to do something to your beautiful hair," I pointed out reluctantly.

"I don't care," she replied, "I'll do anything to atone."

I had no idea what she was talking about, but it was fun cutting her hair. Lily started out clipping in straight lines leaving her hair as distinctively lovely as it already was. "No, no, no," I said, "This is how Starr cuts her hair," and I proceeded to grab large handfuls and just gouge them out.

Lily cried, at first, but soon she got into the spirit and Scout's lovely chestnut hair lay in a pile on the living room floor. All we had to do then was dye the little bit of hair she had left, black, and spike it with gel. The three of us stayed up all night working on Scout's disguise. I tested it out when Chloe woke up that next morning.

"Hey, Cloe. Starr got back last night, see?" I said.

Chloe was half-asleep and hadn't had her coffee yet. She also avoided her stepmother whenever she could. Still, it was encouraging the way she didn't even bat an eye, but said, "Hi Starr" as she headed out to the back porch.

I suggested that we get a little shut- eye, but Scout wanted to try out her disguise. She headed out the front door with Lily and me right behind her. I saw the freakish woman with no nose rushing towards Scout, but I couldn't react in time. Honestly, I didn't even see Bonnie arrive. It wasn't until it was all over that I found out who had tried to stop the one they call Julia.

The hail of bullets that struck them down forced us back inside. I was scrambling to find a safe place to hide when I saw Lily sit back against an interior wall in the lotus position. Her face was serene. I thought about the three of us cutting Scout's hair and talking and having an enjoyable time just minutes ago and I had the weird thought:

"One dead and one mindless in a matter of seconds. I'm the only one left and all I have is a derringer."

I was thinking of the best way to use my one bullet when it suddenly got quiet outside. I looked out and there was Lily, bigger than Dallas, naked as a Jaybird, with a big ass Boa Constrictor wrapped around her. I did a double-take to the spot against the wall where she'd been a second ago, but she was gone.

I was just beginning to think, "Wow she IS a Goddess," when she proved she wasn't. She died. Right there in front of me. I saw it.

I know, the thing about Alys marching out through a hail of bullets to retrieve the body sounds like a typical Alys Loxley drunken yarn, but it's true. She pulled Lily's body in the hut and we put her in the bed. It was there. I know it was.

<u>Witness #2</u>—Chloe Dunnally/Williams

"Aunt Alys wakes up every morning with mysterious scratches, bumps, bruises and cuts all over her body. She blames everyone else, but the fact is, she's what my stepmother, Starr, calls a "falling-down drunk." One of these days, she's going to drown in the pond, but what can you do? Adults are idiots.

Except, of course, for police officers, sir. Yeah, so, we were down at the pond cleaning one of those wounds when the shooting started. When I saw the figure coming out the front door, I really thought it was Starr for a second.

There was something off about her walk, but, as soon as that thought registered, the crazy lady was shooting her at point-blank range with a shotgun. The minute that body hit the ground, Alys went all zombie-like on me. I had to pull her down to cover, she was just standing there. She was mumbling shit like: "Take it back, Sister Agnes, undo it." I was really getting worried about her mental health and shit.

Then I saw something that took my mind off the crazy lady. My crazy boyfriend was driving a jeep right in front of a half-a-dozen blazing rifles. He slammed the brakes of the jeep. He had a big, goofy grin on his face as he grabbed the handles of a big machine gun mounted on a tripod on the back of the jeep.

I jumped up and ran to him. "No, Chris, no! You're going to get hurt!"

The stupid thing wouldn't fire for some reason. Chris looked over my way with a puzzled look on his face, like, "What do I do now?"

He was flung off the back of the jeep by the force of the shot to his arm. He lay in the street and I cradled him in my arms. I was grateful we had been able to have sex once, but I wished it could have been more. Things did not look good.

Then it got quiet. I looked up and there was this huge hologram of Lily dressed up as the goddess Lilith, snake, and all. Alys helped me get Chris inside. After that, I was busy taking care of Chris and I don't know what happened. I was aware when they brought Lily in the hut, but I don't know if she was alive or dead, goddess or human. I just know they put her in the bed.

The blanket that served as a wall was pretty much bullet-riddled, but still provided a modicum of privacy.

Nobody thought of her again until the police were there, and Lucky was trying to explain what happened and pulled back a blanket and said, "She's gone."

<u>Witness #Three- Alys Loxley</u>

The kid came out on the back porch and said those magic words: "It isn't her." I didn't wait for an explanation. I ran out to the front porch and there was Starr, standing over what was supposed to be her dead body.

"Hi," she said.

"Hi!?!" The silly bitch dies, is resurrected, and has nothing better to say than, "Hi"? I ran to her and grabbed her. I held her tight. I vowed to my new God, Lilith that I would never let go.

<u>Witness #4- Starr Williams.</u>

It was the Portland Coven, of course. The tree cover comes right up to the back of the shack. There's a window right there by the window. There were still four or five of them alive. They could have easily taken her body out the window and carried it off.

Why? Well, I can speculate as well as the next girl, but it seems pretty obvious. They want women to believe she is still alive, you know, like Elvis. They intend to start a new cult.

They have their #1 True Believer already. Alys goes on endlessly about how Lilith went back in time and changed history and brought me back to life. It's wonderful to have my relationship with Alys restored but it's a bit of a drag living with a religious fanatic.

Still, I guess I'd really prefer Alys worshipping Lily rather than sneaking off to her bed."

<u>Witness #5 Dawn Hightower-</u> My savior lay bleeding on the ground. I fell to my knees in despair.

"Hark!" I cried, "I have brought thee the head of thy assailant."

"Bless you, my child. Your reward will be to rule my Church on Earth as I will rule in Heaven."

"With that She ascended into the heavens and whosoever will believe on Her (and give me 10% of their earnings) will verily live forever!"

EPILOGUE

Starr and I broke up a year later over a girl named Bessie. They tell me Starr went down at the Battle of Cripple Creek in Lake Charles, Louisiana. They say she took ten men with her, but that doesn't make me feel any better. This old world will not be the same without her.

I suppose it's a good thing I'll be leaving this world soon. The "Army of Righteous Men" as they call themselves, has besieged us here at the Alamo Motel for three days now. Though they outnumber us 10-1, we've killed thrice their number.

We've got nothing left, though. Other than Jen's Bowie knives, all we have are a few pitchforks and some hammers. It'll all be over by this time tomorrow. Still, they will rue the day they took on the Alys's Amazon Auxiliary.

Most of the women who died here the last couple of days followed me into battle. Their blood is on my hands. I was a True Believer. I thought that Lilith had given us permission to decide when a man should die.

Now I know that the pacifists were right. Violence just leads to more violence. War solves nothing. Good God, y'all.

I survived the Battle of Deer Run, but I'm all alone now. Bessie ran off with a drunk named Cassie. Cathy became the Queen of Greenland.

Chloe and Chris are married. They have two kids: Bert and Ernie. Chloe constantly and publicly denounces the church she created as a joke, but it thrives, nonetheless.

Dawn, as its High Priestess, is the picture of respectability with her husband at her side. At night, she dresses like a man and picks up women to spank her.

I won't die an atheist. I believe in the Gods, all of Them. They are there, looking down on us in amusement. When it's time for war, the Gods appoint heroes to fight them, and retire to their own particular Olympus to watch…and to laugh.

Maybe the ones like Anne Baldwin are right: the ones who are involved in secret discussions with men to bring about some sort of compromise. I don't know.

I wish we could go back in time and undo all our mistakes.

But we continue to hurl forward.